"Joyous and lyrical, *Snow Road Station* is an ode to the North, in fact an ode to life itself, and all its possibilities." —Mary Lawson, bestselling author of *A Town Called Solace*

"*Snow Road Station* is an exquisitely etched coming-of-middle-age story. With a touch by turns subtle and sensual, Elizabeth Hay explores the surprising differences—and crucial overlaps—between what we think makes us happy, and what actually does. Along the way, we are drawn imperceptibly into intimacy with characters who reckon with the past in order to remake their own—and perhaps the reader's—notions of what family is." —Ann-Marie MacDonald, bestselling author of *Fayne*

"At the center of this sensitive novel . . . is Lulu, a middle-aged actress who has returned to the hamlet of her youth for her nephew's wedding. . . . Hay makes a case for the simplicity of pleasure: 'All you have to do,' Lulu thinks, 'is put yourself in the way of beauty, put yourself into the incredible swing of it.'" —*The New Yorker*

"A moving novel about ageing and transformation. . . . *Snow Road Station* amazed me." —*Peterborough Examiner*

"Like Elizabeth Strout with Olive Kitteridge and Lucy Barton, Hay has created a fictional world to which she returns, to great effect. Both *His Whole Life* and *Snow Road Station* stand on their own, but there's real pleasure in reading them consecutively and re-encountering the characters at later stages of their lives—and in different lights." —*The Literary Review of Canada*

"In this charming, engaging and eloquent novel, Lulu takes centre stage. . . . Like all of Hay's previous novels, *Snow Road Station* is a gift to be cherished." —*Winnipeg Free Press*

Snow Road Station

A NOVEL

ELIZABETH HAY

VINTAGE CANADA

Published by Vintage Canada, a division of Penguin Random House
Canada Limited, Toronto, in 2024. Originally published in hardcover by
Alfred A. Knopf Canada, a division of Penguin Random House Canada Limited,
Toronto, in 2023. Distributed in Canada and the United States of America
by Penguin Random House Canada Limited, Toronto.

Vintage Canada and colophon are registered trademarks
of Penguin Random House Canada Limited.

www.penguinrandomhouse.ca

Library and Archives Canada Cataloguing in Publication

Title: Snow Road Station : a novel / Elizabeth Hay.
Names: Hay, Elizabeth, 1951- author.
Description: Previously published: Toronto: Knopf Canada, 2023.
Identifiers: Canadiana 20220261032 | ISBN 9781039003347 (softcover)
Classification: LCC PS8565.A875 S66 2024 | DDC C813/.54—dc23

Cover and book design by Kelly Hill
Cover art by Shannon Pawliw
Typeset by Daniella Zanchetta

Printed in Canada

2 4 6 8 9 7 5 3 1

Penguin
Random House
VINTAGE CANADA

with love and gratitude

Martha Kanya-Forstner
Christopher MacLehose

Grow accustomed to the desert
and the star
pouring down its incandescent
rays, which are

just a lamp to guide the treasured
child who's late

Joseph Brodsky, "Lullaby"

Fields go back to forest, first love runs to fat.

Lulu was alone when she left the theatre. In the cold night air beyond the stage door, she replayed that last scene in her mind: the private audience after the audience had left. The sound of him coming down the hall, calling to the four winds, surfing on his own hearty and unstoppable momentum, "Let's see! Let's see if she recognizes my voice!" She had swung around in her chair and there in her dressing room door was Orson Welles gone to wrack and ruin.

"Lu," he grinned, "it's Tony Lloyd."

Milder shocks have turned a person grey overnight. The last time they had been together, in a sailboat on her lake of bays, his hips would have slid into Cinderella's slipper. What a transformation from heartthrob to this: bloated face, shaggy white hair and beard, wild moustache.

"Honey, you're a mess," she said, getting to her feet in amazement. "You should lay off those candy bars."

Laughing, he engulfed her in a hug from their hippie days and her embarrassment burned deeper. "You saw the play," she said, and winced.

But his sheepish smile. "I wanted to. I saw the ad in the *Citizen*, but I had a commitment I couldn't break." He pulled up a chair and settled beside her, resting his hands on her forearms, lightly, in the old way, before letting them fall between his knees. He was bulky in his winter coat, a man out of a tall tale.

She had been crazy about him all those years ago, his way of being a bad boy but kind, living on coffee and cigarettes, wearing jeans without underwear, collecting books but never reading them, disarming her with eager loving that cost him nothing. Had he ever given her a present? Not even at Christmas.

And now they were sixty-two years old and it was snowing again. She raised her collar, turned her back on the dark fortress of a theatre, and headed in the direction of Confederation Park and her hotel. The eerie quiet of downtown Ottawa on a Saturday night in March. Every time she had looked up these last few weeks it was snowing. On her walks to the river, dinning her lines into her head, snow came over her boots. She remembered her mother saying that across the river, in Quebec, they call the snow that falls in March a broom that sweeps away the old snow. What a cunning way to soften the blow of the never-ending accumulation. *This* snow is helping to get rid of *that* snow. *This* broken heart is getting rid of *that* broken heart.

Had she recognized his voice? Only after he began telling her about himself, how he was a businessman based in Asia, "although my business isn't really kosher," he'd chuckled, taking her into his confidence in his old unabashed way.

Listening to him, the play and her humiliation receded. The bare wire of the past touched the bare wire of the present and zapped her heart. 1979 then, 2008 now.

In the park she rested her eyes on the lampposts: snow globes turned upside down, their spotlit cascades sweeping sideways, then dashing down, then up again, then down, riding the nerve ends of every air current. Effortless, she thought. A beautiful performance for an audience of one.

Despite the hour, she too was on the move. Her car was in the hotel's parking lot, her suitcase in the trunk. She wasn't driving back to Montreal, she was escaping to her lake of bays.

Almonte, Middleville, Hopetown—she had known these dots on the map since childhood. The two-lane road curved its way west, gradually rising into the Lanark Highlands. On either side were sloping white fields, up late and reading themselves in the dark. Nan would be awake too, waiting for her, wanting to hear how it went, and what could she say? That she had muffed her lines and it was like falling from a great height: the bottom came up so slowly to meet her. What's the *line*? The last one, yes, but what's the next one? Come *on*. *What's the next line?* Dry mouth, icy hands, the full-on horror of her vision going dark at the edges—as if she were about to faint—and all she had was a strange hyper-focus on not knowing what came next and the audience's growing dismay. "Line! *Line!*" Until the prompter fed her Winnie's next words in a theatre catching on fast. No more nodding off. An actor was coming apart at the seams.

Afterwards, her trusty co-star Ferris jammed his woollen toque on his head and slunk out in his ratty brown jacket without saying goodnight. And it washed over her afresh—the panic and shame, and letting people down. "There's one thing actors have to do," she thought, "and that's remember their fucking lines."

At the foot of the Hopetown hill she turned south and climbed another hill she knew by heart, on past more fields, and what a relief to be driving mile after mile through the countryside away from the blazing confinement of her burial mound on stage. The role of a lifetime, Winnie in Beckett's *Happy Days*, but the director was Richard and they hadn't agreed on anything. "Play it for laughs," he kept saying. "Be funny, Lu. Just decide to be funny."

"*You* be funny," she'd said. Asshole.

"O woe is me." That was the joke of it. Winnie—fishing for dear life in her mud puddle of a brain for the old quotations from school—*Hamlet*, Milton, Keats—desperate for anything to hang on to—terrorized, sun-addled Winnie couldn't remember either.

Alone in the spotlight, buried up to her neck yet still chirping away: the last gasps of a broken bird. Willie was there—Ferris—but she couldn't see him until he crawled into view, dressed to kill, intent on scaling her mound and getting her gun and putting her out of her misery, no doubt. She couldn't play it for laughs, not just for laughs. It should scald the audience, take their heads off, leave them changed, floored, done in. And she thought of *King Lear* in London a few years ago: Cordelia and Lear at the end. How she couldn't get up from her seat after that, not for a long while.

At County Road 8 she swung right through rougher, emptier country to Watson's Corners and Dalhousie Lake, up the long hill past the baseball field to McDonald's Corners with its general store and church and scattering of houses, then windingly and more downhill than not towards Elphin, less hamlet than intersection despite its imposing church. She sensed what lay beyond her in the never-ending dark: the lonely woodlots and woodpiles, the split-rail fences, the rumpled fields interrupted by encroaching cedars, the small simple houses and every so often newer ones—suburban-looking and charmless—the sugar bushes, the bare rock, the unsung Canadian Mississippi. Off the beaten track and with place names peculiar to this part of the world—a village appearing where corners meet.

The falling snow had subsided, the night was clear. Turning north at Elphin, she drove to the hilltop and ahead of her was the full moon flooding the valley with cold glittering light. Halfway down the long descent, the road flattened out before dipping again, then once more: "a nun's pleasure." Another Quebec turn of phrase, but she hadn't learned that one from her mother. At the bottom, the road hugged the edge of Stump Lake and continued on to the bridge over the curving Mississippi, and it was like going from room to room in a dark house without hurting herself, she knew it so well. It was like putting on her slippers and pouring herself a stiff drink.

Now the stone house on the riverbank came into view and Lulu slowed down and pulled over, stopping where she usually did not stop. A tall and handsome landmark she always admired on her way by, having learned to hive it off from memories of being here with Tony. Imagine that: Tony Lloyd showing up again after all these years.

Rolling her window partway down, she sat still for a while, the house and river on her left, the woods on her right.

She had recognized his lips, unchanged behind that slop of beard, as were his attractively crooked teeth. His old in-cahoots smile—surely it was more preening than it used to be. And his voice—more self-satisfied as he filled her in on what had happened after he left her, how he went to Nicaragua to see what a revolution was like and befriended a mercenary who knew Spanish, but the guy turned out to have weapons and drugs in the false bottom of his suitcase, and they were both thrown in jail. "It was terrible. Mock executions, beat-ings. I couldn't set eyes on a gun for a year without bursting into tears."

After which he could see guns by the bucketload without blinking an eye? But she let him ramble on, playing up his innocence and expecting her to buy in. So he went to Asia, "where it would be peaceful," again scanning her face for sym-pathy, admiration even, and there he became a gold smuggler.

No kidding.

To think he thought he was still recognizable. She wanted to grab a pair of scissors and snip the unruly hairs breaking free of his beard, doing handstands beside his nose.

"I was thrown in jail in Asia too," he told her, "six weeks in Hong Kong, nine weeks in India. After that, I told the woman I'd been sleeping with and living with for two years that I wanted love in my life."

Here we go, she thought. We've come to the love part.

"I told Sherry I was going to leave her in six months," he went on without a trace of irony, as if the very model of consideration. "And four months later she was pregnant."

Lulu stared at him, too taken aback to respond. This is you, Tony, she thought. You engineered your own fate, but you can't see it or admit it. You're not responsible for anything. Things just happen to you.

The stone house was dark, moonlit: a house with an actual turret and an air of romance in this Ontario backwoods of scattered cottages, trailers, shacks, farms. She knew what the inside was like too, its formal rooms and curving staircase, because Tony's mother had lived here one winter years ago. Lonely, easygoing Eleanor Lloyd abandoned by her sad-eyed lech of a husband eleven years younger than herself. She was a southerner, from Tennessee like Sam McGee, she used to say, sitting by her woodstove and intoning, "*Please close that door. / It's fine in here, but I greatly fear You'll let in the cold and storm— / Since I left Plumtree, down in Tennessee, it's the first time I've been warm.*"

Eleanor had followed love to the little town of Lanark, half an hour away, and then retreated here to live for a season like a destitute lady of the manor. She would console Lulu by saying her son came by his fecklessness all too naturally.

"Tony," Lulu had said finally. "She outsmarted you. Your Terry."

"Sherry," Tony said. And Lulu smiled.

The theatre had gone quiet, goodnights were being exchanged backstage, and Sal poked her dyed-pink head through the door. "Coming for a drink?"

"Not tonight, Sal." Lulu gestured towards Tony. "Sal, this is Tony Lloyd, a blast from my past."

Tony chuckled again. That really was the same: his devilish, amused-with-himself, belly-deep chortle.

"Sal is our beloved and tireless stage manager," she said to him.

Sal acknowledged the unmade bed of a man with a nod before abruptly turning back to Lulu. "You're not going off to brood over a bowl of soup, are you?"

"Not over a bowl of soup," Lulu said, and eyed the flicker of amusement on Sal's face. "So was he here tonight?"

"Who?"

"Samuel Beckett," she said. "Who do you think? Richard. He was, wasn't he? Did he come backstage?"

"For a minute."

"Did he have any notes for me?"

Sal shook her head. "He talked to Bev."

The assistant stage manager who doubled as prompter. "Bev should have taken a bow, not me," Lulu muttered, and Sal said firmly, "We've got three days off. Wednesday you'll be back on track."

"Every night I'm worse, Sal. I don't know what to do."

Sal leaned against the doorway, sympathetic, businesslike, a little prim. "First, get some sleep."

"I can't sleep."

Sal sighed. "Get some rest then. These next few days are a nice break. It's Easter. Listen to music. Go for walks. Give yourself a full day or two off."

"Beckett. Can't you make it up? Who would know?" Tony said from his chair.

That made Lulu laugh. "Great mercies, small mercies, oh well, what does it matter, soon I'll be dead and buried, woe is me, another *happy* day!"

"Remind me," said Tony. "This isn't the one where the audience sees only a mouth?"

"Nope. I'm buried in sand, roasting under a blistering sun, and all I've got in this hellhole of a desert is the stuff in my handbag and my monosyllabic husband named, of course, Willie. Because that's the kind of fun guy Beckett is."

Sal's gaze sharpened and so did her voice. "Lu, remember, you're a pro. You've got everything you need? Your rehearsal bag?"

"Yes, even the gun. Should I require it."

Sal blew her a light kiss and was gone.

Tony said, "Is she always like that?"

"In a hurry? Yes. She has a lot to do." Lulu said, "I like her. She doesn't fuck people around."

Her eyes rested on Tony for a long moment. She was seeing the scrim of their messy past beyond the recent messiness of the play. Sal was her island of sanity. They had known Richard as a director long enough to watch him burn through half a dozen girlfriends, to see him be brilliant and perverse, play favourites, ruin lives. It irked them both that he spent as much time with Ferris (who only had to crawl around the mound and remember a few lines) as he did with Lulu, when she was the one carrying the play on her back, virtually a two-hour monologue, a mountain of a part. Unbelievably, at the end of an exhausting day in the windowless rehearsal room, Richard had declared that he didn't think *Happy Days* was a very good play.

"It's good," Lulu had said.

"Not Beckett at his best." Pressing his thin lips together.

Well, he was worried. About the production, about his reputation, about her. But then she had been a last-minute replacement, the offer coming out of the blue two months before opening night. "We lost our actor. Would you be interested and available to step in?" And she had leapt at it, thrilled to be wanted and to have work. Only to realize that Richard had thought of her not because of her acting chops, but because she looked like the Winnie he had in mind. Beckett had specified a plump and buxom actress, preferably a blonde in her fifties, so that during the second act, when she's buried up to her neck, the audience will be thinking about her curvaceous flesh and missing it. Richard had dolled her up like a tart, then said, "She's a cockteaser in late middle age, Lu. Face it. Look at yourself." Point of order! Point of order! "Winnie's not a cockteaser, Richard, and I'm not Winnie."

Over the years her method for surviving, now threadbare with use, was to speak her mind, rely on her fellow actors, and treat everybody backstage like gold. Her pal Shawn— who had proved to be more than a pal, as it turned out—had refused to light her as harshly as Richard demanded, so she wouldn't be boiled alive.

"The play's good," she had repeated. "In fact, it's great." And Sal had chimed in with her agreement, dear disciplined Sal who never made things worse for people.

"So where are you living now?" Lulu asked.

"Not far from Bangkok." Tony hunched forward, boyish in his boastfulness if nothing else. "I was happy in Hong Kong until the authorities ran me out of the country."

"And where are you staying in Ottawa?"

Another sheepish look. "With Roseanne," he admitted.

Lulu remembered Roseanne. His old girlfriend from high school. An oversexed cheerleader with fat ankles.

"I'm in Canada a lot," Tony said, "but I can't ever see anyone when I come through because I'm always carrying millions of dollars on my person."

Lulu clocked him waiting for a reaction, she didn't give him one, and he went on. "This time, though, I'm staying through the weekend. Going to some wedding in Lanark. Roseanne's niece is getting married. And anyway, I'd kind of like to see the place I was born. See if they've moved the river."

She leaned back. "We're going to the same wedding. The groom is one of Nan Waterman's sons. Remember Nan? I'm driving to her place tonight."

"Vaguely. Maybe. She lives in Lanark?"

"Snow Road Station."

"Snow Road," he said, lingering on the name.

Her gaze narrowed. "Gold in what form?" Trying to picture it, deciding whether or not to believe him. Wasn't gold heavy? Did he carry it in a suitcase? He didn't look rich, he looked every inch a bum.

"I smuggle bullion," he said simply. "It's money laundering, to be honest. Twice I've had to change my name. Although," he hastened to add, "gold smuggling is a highly respected profession in Asia."

"Who do you work for?" Curious, and wondering if he would tell her.

"My client's in Montreal. I've crossed the country by train so many times, back and forth between Vancouver and Montreal." Finally sounding weary of his life.

How vulnerable he was. How desperate to justify himself and to impress her—to play the romantic rogue when he was just a money-grubbing businessman working off the grid, pulling his innocent-hippie cloak around his unsorry fat bones.

He leaned forward then and placed his rather fine hands on either side of her knee, his old seductive move. "What about you, Lulu? Do you have a stable loving relationship? Are your children good people with loving hearts?"

She rolled her window the rest of the way down and the air was coldest on her ears. Not a sound in the vast quiet. You need a long life, she was thinking, to see how things turn out.

They were on the sailboat again, moving across the lake of bays. His light summer pants slid down on his graceful hips, would have slid off if not held by a belt. The slenderness, first. The lack of vanity, second. Third, the focus given to his hips and crotch by less than reliable material. Slender men whose pants were loose had always attracted her. She remembered him saying to her, Could you try to be more easygoing? Stop caring so much when things don't turn out the way you want them to? And stop badgering me about the future.

Where had the future taken him? "I warned Sherry," he'd said in the dressing room. "This isn't a long-term relationship, so don't fall in love. I stayed with her even though she's disturbed. I couldn't give up my child again. I couldn't do it."

Lulu laid her forehead on the cold steering wheel, letting that sink in a second time. "*My* child," she had said.

"Our child." And he had touched her knee again.

"In what way is Sherry disturbed?" was all she said, not sorry they weren't happy, but sorry about everything else.

"Well, someone who sleeps around in Asia isn't going to be stable. She has no empathy. She's selfish. *I've* been the mother to my two sons."

Lulu said nothing, tired of him and too sad for words. He hadn't asked a single thing about her own life and wouldn't, not until his innocent killer of a question at the end: Were her children good people with loving hearts? To which she had shrugged, not caring to admit there were no children, none. Instead, getting to her feet, she had said she could talk all night but she had miles to go before she slept.

"I have sleeping pills if you want them," he offered, heaving himself out of his chair, wrapping her in another hug. "You said you can't sleep. I get them in India. You can't get them here."

"On your person?" Her lips twitched. "You've got them on your person?"

"In my suitcase."

"Well, if you think I'm going with you to Roseanne's you've got another think coming."

"I'll bring them to the wedding," he promised.

Raising her forehead from the steering wheel, she felt the ache in her neck shoot across her upper back and do a little number below her left shoulder blade. Buried up to her chin for the whole of the second act, free to move her lips and swivel her eyes and that's it. Winnie's brave, ridiculous song at the end. "*Though I say not / What I may not / Let you hear / Yet the swaying / Dance is saying / Love me dear!*"

Maybe she was trying too hard, that's why she was losing her lines. Maybe her old jalopy for brains had blown a gasket and she was rolling back downhill, misfiring as she went, like Jack and Jill, she thought, and here they were in a heap at the bottom. Probably she looked as old and unrecognizable to Tony as he did to her. Somebody you worried about. Somebody off the rails.

A set of headlights loomed up behind her.

The car slowed down as it passed and pulled over twenty yards ahead. She drew her bag close. Deep countryside and people looked out for each other, especially in wintertime, but you never know. The driver limped towards her in his duffle jacket. Maybe a grizzled director scouting snow scenes for his next movie. Sydney Pollack or Kiarostami or Clint Eastwood. The old fantasy. Lulu Blake, pulled over on the side of the road; and sexy old Clint seeing her behind the wheel, discovering the very face he had been searching for high and low.

The stranger leaned down and looked in at her open window. "You okay? Can I help?"

Bareheaded. An older man, not tall, not at all bad-looking, with a nose that bent to the right. Rugby player, she thought.

"I'm fine. Everything's fine. But thanks for checking on me."

"I thought you might be lost," he said.

"I know exactly where I am."

He nodded. An open face. Deep-set, interested, very tired eyes.

She waved her hand grandly towards what lay beyond. "*The woods are lovely, dark and deep.*"

"*But I have promises to keep,*" he returned with a smile, "and so on and so on. Then I'm not going to have you on my conscience? You're all right?"

"Never better." In that moment it was true. She was astonished at how a little mild flirtation set her to rights.

He limped back to his car and drove on, and Lulu had the night to herself again, the silence and the cold. Once again it was snowing, a sight that never failed to bring her peace of mind along with wakefulness. A thick curtain of snow had been climbing her hotel window in Ottawa for weeks. And now something else flashed white before her eyes: the sign-out sheet on the callboard she had forgotten to fill in. No one involved in the play knew where she was right now. She hadn't even told Sal about the wedding. I could walk into the dark woods and never be seen again.

Well, she would phone Sal once she got to Nan's. Tomorrow. Or the next day.

In the meantime, being AWOL might have its charms. In her headlights thousands of snowflakes were whirling in all directions, an exotic tumble, sallying this way and that in the buoyant air. She reached up and angled the rear-view mirror to take a look at what her limping man had seen. A lot of mileage, she thought. Or these days a lot of kilometrage. A lot of kilometrage in that face. "Honey, you're a mess," she said out loud. The plain truth stared her in the eyes.

We don't remember things, she thought, and it's not because we've forgotten. They're in hiding, waiting to leap out and do us in. Suddenly faced with Tony like that. It was like coming upon a coat at the back of her closet, a big enveloping garment she used to love, yet once out of sight, amazingly it was out of mind. Now here it was again. Sliding the memory off its hanger, she marvelled at the weight, buried her face in its folds, felt a surge of the old, old longing.

She was rolling up her window when a scream tore through the night air and her hand stopped in mid-motion. High-pitched, piercing, ending in a wail of despair. A life being snuffed out.

Only one, deep in the woods. Claws sinking into something soft and a bloody triumphant beak.

That's something you never forget, how to scream. Winnie lets rip three times in the second act and her own screams were first-rate. Not even Richard complained about her screams.

She was eleven years old, reading in the corner of the kitchen, when her mother came inside saying she had heard a banshee. She looked up to see her mother's ashen face and the answering fear in her father, the pair of them rooted to the spot and speechless. The next day a police car pulled into the laneway, and her parents were too petrified to get up from the table. She was the one who went to the door. The officer stepped inside and told them how sorry he was, but their son Bernie had drowned in the Klondike River.

Rolling her window shut, Lulu pulled back onto the road. Soon the cedars on her right gave way to big old maples around a sugar shack. The sight was something from an earlier time and for her always ushered in the beginning of Snow Road Station.

Snow was a man. The road was named after its surveyor, not the weather, a fact that disappointed at first, until the idea of it became more tolerable, or at least inevitable, and the name's meaning expanded all over again. Snow Road Station was an arrival, a departure, a long wait—a place of rest, a stoppage, yet a road.

The name was like a poem, she thought, or a three-act play. A passenger arrives in the snow with her southern accent and broken heart. Her son and his girlfriend come to visit, weighed down by their pressing problem. A decision is made. People part. The station closes, the railway tracks get torn up, no more train whistles to listen for.

But the name persists. Years ago in New York, a young actor came to her for voice lessons, and Lulu asked her where she was from. "You wouldn't know it," the girl replied. "It's just a little place in Ontario."

"Try me, darling."

"Snow Road Station," came the answer. A farm girl from one of the maple syrup families that still maintained a sugar bush of thousands of trees. There had been a time when more maple syrup was shipped from Snow Road Station than from anywhere else in Canada. Lulu had hugged her like a long-lost friend.

Snow

1

IN THE LANE her headlights picked out sparks flying up into the darkness and the glint of sap buckets on trees. Two figures were moving about in the light cast from the side porch as if on their own stage set, a hideaway in the woods. The porch, wide and screened-in, ran the full width of the two-storey house which overlooked the lake of bays.

Lulu parked and called out, "You're peaches to wait up for me." She went forward and hugged Nan, whose clothes and hair smelled of maple and woodsmoke. Her old friend was thin and sinewy, tree and axe in one. Young Ducky, Lulu's niece, was more like her own full-bodied self.

"Ducky, and now you," Nan cried, helping Lulu take the bags out of her car and inside. "Soon Jim will be here too. Any moment now, I hope."

Nan's sugar camp at the side of the house had basic props and nothing more: a cast-iron woodstove with two large pans of bubbling sap sending up clouds of steam, a wooden table bearing a soup pot and ladle, several outdoor chairs, several big white plastic buckets, a blue barrel of fresh sap, a rake and shovel, and a lean-to of split firewood within easy reach. The floor was packed snow, the ceiling was treetops and sky. Soon Nan was offering Lulu a ladleful of sap and the sweetness wafted up to Lulu's nose, bringing with it the childhood memory of sap icicles and sap gathering. And then the taste. Very light. Like tasting apple blossoms, thought Lulu.

The last time she had been here was at Christmas, when Ducky too had come for a few days. But summers were their usual time at the lake.

Now Nan was pulling a bottle out of the snow and Lulu smiled—champagne was the one drink she never turned down. They must be robbing the wedding supply. And they were like mother and daughter, she thought, as Ducky held out the glasses and Nan poured. It wasn't quite fair, Nan with her two sons and Guy's daughter a regular too. Yet how happy they were to see her, and she them.

Lulu had been five years old, riding in her mother's lap, the first time they turned off at Snow Road Station and came down the lake road. One of their rare treks from the Yukon to Ontario before moving back here for good. In the back seat of the car Bernie and Guy leaned out either side and threw up. Her mother had granted them sticks of gum to steady their stomachs on the narrow dirt roller coaster whose ups and downs and long, reaching curves brought into view the wide surprise of hilly pastures dotted with boulders and with bunches of trees like roughly gathered bouquets. Wooden split-rail fences zigzagged beside roads and fields—and Lulu recalled riding like a queen with the best view of all and *she* wasn't throwing up. The road led to her great-uncle's farm at a bend in the lake, where she would learn how to swim, rivers in the Yukon being too cold and dangerous, fatal in fact, while this lake was ideal, an island-studded stretch of deep blue water.

The farm with its sugar bush was her brother Guy's now, but tonight she had carried on past it, following the curves to Nan's house with its field in front, and woods at the side, and steep slope down to the lake. There were places in the world where she felt close to how things would be if they were allowed to be themselves, and the lake road was one and the lake itself another.

They clinked glasses. "To Winnie," said Nan. "Long live Samuel Beckett and you."

Ducky joined in. "To you and *Happy Days*. I'd give anything to see it."

"Lulu's terrific," said Nan. "Lu, you *are* the play."

Well, Nan had come on opening night, before she started to unravel. But all Lulu said was, "You really are peaches to spoil me this way."

The trees were excited too, she thought, looking around her at the tapped maples peeing like pregnant women, flowing like nursing mothers, wet like a harem constantly aroused.

"I'm up at five," Nan was saying, "and it's magical. No wind. Nothing but chickadees singing as I get the fire going and gather the sap. This morning I saw a shooting star."

"Darling, you make me sick," Lulu said, settling herself into one of the chairs and nestling her glass in the snow. She held her hands out to the stove. "Speaking of saps, a man came back into my life tonight. Do you remember Tony Lloyd?"

"Tony Lloyd." Nan was all attention. "I haven't seen him in years."

"Believe it or not, he'll be at the wedding, tagging along with Roseanne."

"What's he doing now?"

"He smuggles gold."

"Gold?"

"So he claims. I should have asked more questions. Not that I would have believed his answers."

Nan leaned forward and said with conviction, "He was a *very* sexy man."

Her ringing endorsement stirred up distant memories and Lulu was walking with him down the railway bed again, lost in their predicament: he didn't want to be a father, she was an actress living hand to mouth. And now she was still living hand to mouth and whenever he landed in jail he wasn't worried, unlike that time in Nicaragua, because he had plenty of money and could buy his way out. His politics, he had freely admitted, were very conservative. He agreed with gunning down the protesters in Tiananmen Square and jailing all the dissenters ever since. "Stability," he had said, "is all that matters."

A man's character changes and he becomes himself. Lulu had read that somewhere, surprised by the turn of thought. Not that he changes and becomes someone else. He becomes the person he's meant to be. What would it take? she wondered. Becoming who you're meant to be, instead of turning into a major disappointment. She raised her eyes and followed the clouds of steam rising to mingle with the smoke from the stovepipe-chimney and wafting up into the dark branches burdened by their snow-petal load. A glimpse of the reappearing moon, and she recalled a night like this years ago when she had built a snow fort with Ducky and Guy, constructing a tunnel and two rooms, making windowpanes from frozen sheets of coloured water. It was one of the happiest nights of her life, their exuberant mood and the abundant snow filling the sad holes in her heart and reconciling her to her brother. She and Guy had not spoken a mean word to each other since.

"When did you say Jim was arriving?"

"He should have been here an hour ago." Nan rubbed her forehead with her gloved hand.

"*He's* a sexy man. Right, Ducky?" And Lulu's niece lived up to her nickname by ducking behind her hair.

Women in love, Lulu thought, older women too. The sap still flows. She was thinking of the blue-haired women of her youth, who, in league with the tight-lipped librarian, hogged all the Harlequins. She was thinking of herself.

A clump of snow slid from an overhead bough into the open pan without making a sound.

"You've gone quiet," Nan said to Lulu. "What is it?"

Theirs was a childhood friendship that had lasted, enduring long spells when it existed out of sight, but then there it was again, like strawberries in season.

"Lu?"

Her eyes had filled with tears. She gave her head a shake, coughed, cleared her throat. "This is lovely," she said, gazing down at the champagne. Just what the doctor ordered. "Are you ready for the wedding?"

Nan sighed. "What a mistake."

Ducky, alert and interested, spoke up in her clear voice. "You think they're wrong for each other?"

"Why do we complicate our lives by marrying the wrong people?" Nan got to her feet and reached for the ladle and stirred.

"I did the same thing," she went on. "In fact, I did it twice. He's wrong for her. He's going to make her very unhappy." Her discouraged voice silenced them for a while, until Ducky said, "What were your wrong weddings like?" And Lulu smiled.

"Funerals," Nan said. "I married John Sharpe when I was in love with someone else who was already married. Well, it was your father. But you knew that." She paused. "Am I embarrassing you?"

Ducky's eyes didn't leave Nan's face. "Go on."

This was old news but still fascinating: Nan's revelation eight years earlier that her youthful affair with Guy, when he was married and she was not, had produced her son Blake. At twenty-four, Blake had learned that he was not, after all, John Sharpe's son, as his mother had led everyone to believe.

"And then I married George," Nan said. She gave up stirring and settled back into her chair. "He was gentle and I felt sorry for him, but when we said our vows I hyperventilated and nearly passed out."

They fell silent again until Lulu thought to ask if there were wedding preparations she could help with, and Nan said yes. She could help ice and assemble the cake. Six round layers, two layers per tier, plus a back-up sheet to make sure there was enough for all seventy-five guests; she had been baking since yesterday. "We'll assemble it tomorrow afternoon." Nan counted off the days on her fingers. "Tomorrow's Sunday. Well, it's Sunday now. The wedding's Monday at four o'clock. We'll go early to drop off the cake at the community hall." She said, "And I've got my speech to figure out. They want the mother of the bride and the mother of the groom to do the speeches. Keep the confusing fathers out of it."

Catching sight of the moon again, thinking about ill-starred romances, Lulu planted the question that would keep them occupied into the next day and the next. "So," she said, "what *is* it that makes a man sexy?"

"The eyes," Ducky said immediately. "The way he looks at you."

Ducky knows, thought Lulu. "A look of persistent, intense interest," she agreed.

"That pins you down and makes you feel powerless," Ducky said.

"I wouldn't say powerless. At first it gives you a sense of power. Later, when you're hooked, you might feel powerless."

"Vulnerable," Ducky said, and they nodded at each other. "Inadequate," Ducky said. And Lulu eyed her niece and took issue: "My darling, any man who makes you feel inadequate, leave him. Promise me that. Cross your heart and hope to die."

Ducky promised.

Then Lulu turned to Nan, drawing her in, "What about you?" And Nan directed her smile at Ducky, "Your father is still a sexy man."

"The older my brother gets the better looking he is. It's disgusting," said Lulu.

"Did he tell you he injured his neck a couple of weeks ago?" Nan said. "He can't sleep for more than an hour at a time. Julie made him go for acupuncture."

"What did he do to himself?"

"Nothing. He got out of his truck."

"My poor Dad." Ducky got up and tended to the fire, unlatching the door of the stove, chucking more wood into the flames. "And poor Julie. He's a terrible patient." The flames lit up her face and Lulu was struck by how young and lovely she was, a girl in her last year of high school. She remembered the silent four-year-old spending August here with her father before returning to her city-loving mother in Toronto, Guy's second wife. By the age of nine she had turned into a racy dresser doing cartwheels in the laneway, and at thirteen she blew everyone away when she played Leontes in *The Winter's Tale* at Lulu's theatre camp.

"*Is whispering nothing?*" Lulu said now.

And Ducky turned and took up the challenge, "*Is leaning cheek to cheek? Is meeting noses? / Kissing with inside lip?*"

"*Why, then the world and all that's in't is nothing,*" said Lulu.

"*My wife is nothing; nor nothing have these nothings,*" Ducky said, "*If this be nothing.*"

"You're a natural, my Ducky," said Lulu, delighted with her and not a little relieved that she too could remember the lines. She didn't spoil the mood by confessing her warring memories of *The Winter's Tale*: hearing her high school English teacher read out those very words and feeling herself thrill in response, then years later actually reading the play from start to finish, and thinking, What is this junk? Is everyone out of their minds except me? Later still, in search of material for the camp she had run on Guy's farm until it closed for lack of customers, she finally agreed the play had great moments. Nevertheless, sometimes Shakespeare stank. Maybe as an actor too. Maybe he was an actor the way he was a writer, either brilliant or bad, or both in the same play. She knew actors like that. Probably she was one herself.

But not her fabulous niece. Seventeen years old and auditioning for theatre schools, and Lulu wouldn't dream of discouraging her. But how could she help her be strong and realistic in the face of all the rejection and malice out there? "You look exquisite, Ducky, do you know that?" And Ducky blushed with pleasure.

Jim was coming home, that's what it was. She was waiting for Jim. "Jim's coming from Boston?" said Lulu.

Nan had been glancing at her watch and now she covered her wrist with her hand and nodded. He was flying into Ottawa and renting a car. "I wish he'd call. He must think we're asleep."

"He'll get here soon," Lulu said.

To distract Nan from morbid thoughts, she added, "Also the voice." And pushing herself out of her chair, she recalled Tony's confiding, jocular, subversive patter and his laughter halfway between a chuckle and a snicker. "And I can't get enough of a man's hips."

She was preparing the ground, it would dawn on her later, setting palm leaves of desire under her feet.

"I also like a pair of bowed legs," she said.

Ducky let out a yelp. "So do I!"

"Slightly bowed," Lulu emphasized. "From behind and wearing jeans." Searching the perimeter of the stove, she spotted what she was after. "There's nothing like sitting around a campfire to give your soul a rest, but I'm starving and I'm taking this with me." She pulled the half-full bottle out of the snow.

2

NAN'S BIG COUNTRY kitchen, warmed by its own wood-stove, had a long trestle table next to a bank of windows. On one end of the table were seven cakes, still in their pans, giving off an aroma that fuelled Lulu's rampaging hunger. She set about plundering cupboards and drawers. It was after one in the morning.

"Soon you'll be eating like me," she said to Ducky, when she and Nan came inside with the soup pot half-full of near-syrup. Nan would finish it in the morning, reheating and filtering it before pouring it into bottles. "After a performance, not before." By now Lulu had pasta boiling in a pot, while in a frying pan she was stirring a serious amount of garlic and salt in a deep bath of olive oil.

Beside her, Nan reached into a lower cupboard for a tray, which she arranged with plates and cutlery and serviettes—the

bread, the butter—deft and unhurried—and Lulu remembered Nan's brother, Tom Waterman, working with his hands
in the same soothing and exacting way. She turned back to
the stove and watched the garlic soften in the hot oil. "I forgot
my lines tonight," she said.

Nan stopped. "That happens," she said carefully.

"Five fucking times," Lulu said.

It was like doing backflips into the void. The first time
was during the first matinee: an audible pop in her brain
and everything fell away, every word wiped out. By then the
adrenalin of opening night—making it through against all
the odds—had worn off and doubts crept in, wielding their
little knives. A bad review in the *Citizen*, a fishy-eyed look
from the set designer, a sickening sense that she was losing
ground with every performance and horribly there was still
a week left of the three-week run to confirm what a loser
she was.

"The night I saw it you were letter-perfect," Nan said.
"Nobody who saw the play will remember you forgot a few
lines."

"That's *all* they'll remember," Lulu said.

"You got a standing ovation," Nan reminded her.

"Everything gets a standing ovation in Ottawa." Besides,
the standing ovations had come and gone.

Funny how long it takes for all that's troubling you to
reach the surface. Lulu's short bitter laugh had Nan shooting
her another glance. "What?" Nan said.

"Oh, a woman came to see me a week ago. She asked if
we could talk somewhere private, so I brought her into the

green room and sat her down, and she said, 'You don't know my name. You've never seen me before.'" Lulu widened her bemused eyes for effect. "She fished a card out of her pocket and handed it to me. It was my own business card and I'd written on the back. 'I love to play.'"

Nan and Ducky stood riveted, an audience in the palm of her hand.

"She told me, 'I'm marrying Shawn Phillips in a month and I found this card in his backpack on Sunday night.' They'd had a big fight over it. She said to me, 'I haven't eaten, I haven't slept.'"

Nan said, "Who's Shawn Phillips?"

"The lighting guy for the play. So I reassured her. It was nothing, we were nothing to each other. I advised her not to tell him about coming to see me, I even asked her about the wedding." Lulu paused. "I walked her out to the stage door and you know what she said to me? 'Thank you. You've made a younger woman very happy.'"

"What a shit," Nan breathed.

Ducky said, "You should have spat in her face." She pushed her hair behind her ears. "The biggest asshole in my school is called Shawn. Maybe there's something about the name?"

"You wait," Lulu said. "He'll be knocking on my door in six months." He'll be back for his sexy old broad, his juicy Lucy, his queen of the Nile. Or not, she thought. Or not.

It was nearly two o'clock and still no Jim. Nan kept nodding off in her chair, but refused to go to bed. Ducky was wide awake and Lulu was hungry again. Her first time tasting maple syrup, she told them, was having a small bowl of it for dessert when her mother insisted it had to be eaten with a slice of bread. Taking the hint, Nan roused herself. Soon Lulu was dipping a corner of her bread until it was so saturated it could hold no more. Chewing and dipping, she ruminated aloud. "It's pitiful. I'm an aging actor who keeps looking for love."

Nan said, "Why should it be pitiful? Aging men love themselves for going after love."

"I'm a fool."

"They can't get enough of themselves," Nan said.

"I'm old enough to know better."

"Lulu, Lulu. Are you listening to me?"

But Lulu's face was all screwed up, twisted like a wrenched ankle. She couldn't shake her sense of failure, the place deep in her chest that had given up or was wanting to give up.

"I'm thinking of a little face work," she said. And ran her hand across her mouth.

"Oh, Lulu."

Her hand smelled sweet and smoky. It must be on my clothes too, she thought, and in my hair.

"If you want to look old," Nan said, "have a face lift." Then her own face lit up, and pushing back her chair she strode to the porch door and flung it open. But it wasn't Jim who appeared. It was Blake.

He looked almost as disappointed as his mother. "Jim's not here yet? I've been driving around."

How alike they looked, mother and difficult son. Blue-eyed, skinny-intense, dishwater-blond, although Blake's shoulders were broad and he was very pale, while Nan's face was tanned from living in the out-of-doors. They were barely on speaking terms, these two. Blake had told his mother about his wedding by mailing her an invitation from down the road in Lanark. But now the wedding was upon them and here he was.

He kicked off his boots, hung his coat on a peg beside the door, joined them at the table. A man in his early thirties, moody, broody, and handsome. He nodded at Ducky and Lulu, then slumped into the chair across from them and flung one arm behind him, as slim and carelessly graceful, Lulu thought, as Tony used to be.

"We're getting an early start," she said to him. A whiff of cigarette had come in on the winter air. "There's a drop left." Tilting the champagne bottle in his direction.

"I thought Jim would be here," he said.

"The bridegroom can't sleep," she observed. And his mother said, "What's keeping you awake?" Instantly concerned.

Blake's limp hair fell into his eyes. It could use a good wash, Lulu thought, but maybe that's how it looked after a good wash. He was a blend of Nan and her brother Guy, but morose and much more confrontational in his born-again life as an evangelical preacher. She would have cast him as Iago or Angelo, a blend of hot and cold, an agitated man *whose blood is very snow-broth*, and Nan as some gaunt queen who's in the dark.

"Mainly, I lie awake thinking everything I've done in my life I've done wrong."

Ducky said, "I do that too."

Blake studied her. "You're sixteen."

"I am not. I'm seventeen."

He smiled and the difference was night and almost-day. "I hardly remember seventeen," he said, rubbing the back of his neck and staring down, as if he wanted nothing more than to pick his younger self up off the floor and start over.

"Are you sure this is what you want?" his mother said.

He raised his eyes. "What do you mean?"

Nan ran her hand across her forehead, evidently trying to find the right words.

"What?" he said.

She shook her head. The air in the room was prickly from strain and fatigue and Blake.

Then Nan removed her glasses and set them on the table. "If you don't want to get married, say so. It's not too late."

Blake turned his face away.

She said, "You don't have to get married. You could—"

"Bethany's pregnant," he said.

His mother leaned back. She didn't speak for a moment. "And you're sure the baby is yours?"

He stared at her and she held his gaze.

"You would ask that," he said.

"It's not an unimportant question."

"Given your history," he said.

Nan turned her face to the window. "So you're sure?"

"I'm sure."

She sighed. "I remember warning Jim. Did I never warn you?"

"You never told me anything," Blake said.

The room was quiet. The fire in the woodstove had settled into itself.

"Do her parents know?"

"Just us," he said, getting up and making for his coat, heading off any more questions. The wedding rehearsal would be at three. He would call Jim in the morning, he told them.

3

LULU WAS STILL awake, going over lines in her head. By now it was nearly four o'clock. She and Ducky were in the living room, stretched out on opposite ends of the sofa under blankets Nan had spread over them. Lulu always slept poorly when she was playing a role, during the rehearsals and during the run, and afterwards too, in the torture chamber of second thoughts. Tonight, for the first time in two months, she didn't have her script under her pillow or a pile of books about Beckett beside her bed. She prayed that Sal was right, that a break from it all would do her good. Wrapped in a blanket of her own, Nan had fallen asleep in the rocking chair.

If only they had had several months to rehearse instead of a few weeks, if only the play had a year to run instead of less than a month, then she would have stood a chance. The

old style, as Winnie liked to say, when theatres had touring
companies and time. But she couldn't have said no to such a
role. She had never said no. Not in the beginning when parts
were plentiful, not now when they weren't. Because there
was always the hope that this time she would be great, this
time she would dazzle. She was a gambler too, she thought,
a chancer like Tony, taking risks when they were young, still
taking risks.

She lay quiet, thinking about soon-to-be-married Blake,
thinking back to when she and Tony had made a different decision: to end a pregnancy rather than prolong it. She wasn't so
much thinking, however, as communing with old thoughts;
having what Beckett called profounds of mind.

She heard Jim's light tread on the porch steps. He entered
the kitchen, setting his bag on the floor. They had left the
porch light on for him, and a light above the stove. Lulu heard
him take off his coat and boots, and watched him come into
the living room in his stocking feet. He crossed to his mother
and put his hand gently on her shoulder.

Nan opened her eyes. "You're here," she said, and reached
for his hand.

"Don't get up," he whispered.

She was already up. She had her arms around him. "Jim,
you're so *thin*."

Jim wrapped his arms around his mother and pressed his
lips to the side of her head. He was younger than Blake by
seven or eight years. They were half-brothers in more ways
than one: Jim half as guarded as Blake, Blake half as affection-
ate as Jim.

He saw that Lulu was awake too, and went over to her and planted a kiss on her cheek. "Darling," she said, "we've been waiting for you."

Nan was heading to the stove, jabbing her wet eyes with her knuckles. "You'll be hungry."

"I am," he agreed, following her, keeping his voice low. "My flight was so late the car rental was closed. It took an hour for the guy to come. You've still got so much snow," he marvelled.

"Heaps." Lulu spoke behind him. "It's been that kind of winter. We've had Rubenesque piles of snow. Piles? Bellies, bottoms, breasts, hips, thighs. I'm starving," she said.

Nan was filling the coffee pot. "We've had eleven feet. If you look for the picnic table outside, you won't find it."

A voice said, "You made it." Ducky was standing in the kitchen doorway, her blanket around her shoulders.

Jim went to her and lifted her off her feet in a bear hug. "You," he said.

They tucked into eggs and buttered toast and coffee. Nan told Jim the piano tuner was coming in the morning around eleven, even though it was Sunday, so he would have a tuned piano to play. "Not Lex. He's back in Boston. A guy from Snow Road." She paused. "Blake came by a few hours ago, looking for you."

Young Ducky said gravely, "He's having a nervous breakdown."

Jim smiled, concerned, and his mother said, "He needs his best man to shore him up."

"Okay."

"He's depressed, so he doesn't trust his judgment." She wrapped both hands around her mug. "The wedding rehearsal's this afternoon at three."

"Maybe he won't show up for his wedding," Ducky said. "You'll have to hunt him down. Or maybe the bride will take off with an old boyfriend, and Blake will have to hunt *them* down."

Lulu murmured, "Somebody's been reading *Blood Wedding*."

"What a daring play," Ducky said dreamily. "In the end her lover *dies*."

"He'll show up," Nan said.

Lulu rebuttered her buttered toast to the edge and beyond. "Someone I met once—she was married—locked eyes with another woman at a party and that was it, that was the end of family life."

"That would never happen to me," Nan said. "Not with a woman, not with a man. Maybe with a dog. I'd take a dog home."

They retreated in order to get some sleep, Jim to his old room off the kitchen, the others to the three bedrooms upstairs. They were up again by ten.

Lulu knew she should turn on her phone and call Sal, but something in her resisted, just as sometimes she put off learning lines until it took a superhuman effort to sit down with the script. Tomorrow, she thought. Let today be a day of rest.

Gathered in the kitchen, they were talking about the wedding when the piano tuner arrived, and Lulu had to smile. This had happened so many times: a person she had taken note of in passing reappeared in her life. He wasn't as old as she had thought and he held himself well. Nan hung his duffle jacket on a peg by the door, and he limped into the kitchen carrying his leather bag of tools. And maybe it was the morning light or the lack of sleep, but my God what a dreamboat with his surprised face and smashed-crooked nose.

His start of recognition gave way to a broad smile. "So you found your way," he said to her.

She stretched out her hand. "I'm Lulu Blake."

"Hugh Shapiro." Setting down his bag, taking her hand in both of his.

"We were on the road at the same time last night," she explained. "I was on my way here."

"And I was heading home. Did you see the deer?" he said.

"No."

"It was just ahead of us, running alongside the road, looking for a way into the woods."

She shook her head.

"It bounded back onto the road a few times before it found its way into the sugar bush. I thought maybe you saw its tracks."

"I heard a banshee," she said. "You didn't hear it?"

"You must be Irish," he said, and Lulu admitted with a laugh that her mother was half-Irish, half-French: an Irish-Quebecer.

"My grandfather Saul believed in the evil eye," Hugh said with relish, running his hand through what was left of his sandy hair. "He tied a red ribbon around my wrist when I was three years old to keep the evil eye from turning me into a girl. That's how pretty I was."

Lulu thought it was something she didn't see often enough: dry, freckled lips paired up with such tired, amused eyes.

"What's a banshee?" Ducky wanted to know. "Don't tell me. It's what wails outside your house when somebody's about to die."

"It wasn't wailing outside this house," Lulu said.

"But we heard something," Ducky said. "Didn't we?"

Hugh said to Lulu, "You don't really believe you heard a banshee."

"I believe everything," Lulu said.

His amused face stayed in her mind after he followed Nan into the living room and began to tune the piano, repeatedly striking the same key or the ones next to it, up and down. Now he was on the highest keys. Now the lowest. Now in the middle. She pictured the deer plunging into the deep snow, swerving back to the easier road, confused by the headlights and full of strong, fearful life—and as sometimes happened, although never often enough—she saw it as a scene playing out—the past spooling out behind her and the future spooling ahead—direction and crisis and resolution: the welcome salvation of the sugar bush.

Nan had returned from the living room and refilled their coffee mugs. They were all bleary-eyed, especially Jim.

"What about you, Jim?" Lulu said, weaving him into their earlier conversation. "What do you find sexy?"

He stared into the space above the table.

"You're sorry you're here," she said, taking his silence for embarrassment. "A pair of old women, one of them your mother. Ducky's sorry too."

Ducky was watching Jim.

But Jim had always had time for Lulu, and did not dismiss the question or ask where it came from. "Self-awareness," he said.

"That's interesting," Lulu said.

"Not confidence?" his mother said.

"Most confident people aren't self-aware." He said, "I think Emma Bovary is sexy."

"*She's* not self-aware," his mother said.

"She's hungry for what she doesn't have," Jim said.

His singular thought hung in the air until Hugh Shapiro began playing something so affecting they went into the living room the better to listen.

"More," Lulu urged when he came to the end.

"Chopin," he said. "Prelude 4. It's a good party piece when you want to impress somebody."

"We were talking about what makes a person sexy." Lulu held his glance, gauging his reaction. "Research," she deadpanned. "We're actors, Ducky and I."

He didn't miss a beat. "I used to be a fat man," he said. He was solid but muscled. "Then I read a book."

"There are so many." She was thinking of all the dieting books beside her bed. "Maybe I've read it too."

"It was about me," he said. "By a woman I knew. We lived together in California when I was young and fit, and afterwards she wrote about me. Well, about her. About us."

The wedding and the play fell away. He was telling them the story of his life and Lulu didn't even wonder why. They were in the right place at the right time. A cold morning, but warm and comfortable inside with the woodstove sending out heat and someone new in her life taking her mind off her troubles.

"She was looking for me," he said wryly, "trying to track me down. She wrote a book about a sexy man in California, and I was a fat man here."

"So you lost weight," Lulu pointed out.

"A woman finds a man attractive and tells the world in a book. It's worth holding on to the illusion."

He was an American, then. Of course he was. An open American face with nothing to hide. "What's the title of the book?" Lulu asked.

"Oh, it's out of print."

"You bought up all the copies?" It was Nan's turn to smile.

Hugh laughed. Here he was, enchanting them, a Californian who had washed up on colder shores. The area around Snow Road Station was sprinkled with imports like him from south of the border looking for peace and quiet; plus escapees of all ages from big-city life; plus locals who had moved away years earlier, then found their way back to live alongside those who had never left, who farmed, hunted, cut wood, had their pianos tuned, made maple syrup by the gallon.

So all you need, Lulu thought later, is a piano and a good story.

"Women don't let go," Hugh observed, not in a mean way but as common wisdom personally observed.

"Men do?" Nan said. "I wonder if she's thinking about you now as much as you're thinking about her."

He gave her a steady look, unoffended. "You remind me of her," he said.

"Me?"

They could see disbelieving Nan take stock of herself—greying hair, baggy sweater, glasses.

"She was bony too," he said.

"Good one," Nan said, visibly relieved to be off the hook. But he put her back on by saying, "I've always liked a bony, good-looking woman."

"Oh, for heaven's sake," she said. And changing the subject she asked him for his opinion of her piano.

"It's—how can I say? Not a bad piano. I don't want to be dismissive. One of my mentors in New York said you want an iron fist in a velvet glove. A piano has a voice. A strong fundamental tonal centre. When the hammers get hard, the fundamental disappears. With your piano there's only so much I can do to voice it up." He said, "So I say: enjoy your piano and know it doesn't sound bad."

"Okay," Nan said. "About pianos you're honest."

There were some fine pianos in Lanark County, he told her. "I tuned a nice little German upright the other day and it sounded like God's own voice. You want a piano that draws you in. You sit down and you can't stop playing."

"My son's the one who plays." Turning to Jim, "If I had a better piano, would you come home more often?"

Jim smiled an awkward smile and there was silence until Hugh Shapiro said, "Suppose I let you know if I hear of a good piano for sale?"

Jim put his arm around his mother's shoulders. "If you would."

Lulu would have given anything in that moment to have a son like Jim.

He and his mother went back into the kitchen, and Ducky followed. But Lulu stayed where she was, beside the piano, as Hugh began noodling another tune. His hands were nicked here and there on the knuckles, and stained around the nails with blue paint. The tune was familiar, but she couldn't place it. Minor chords going down, that's what made it so sad and unforgettable.

"Christoph Gluck," he told her. "Orpheus singing his sorrows."

He smelled of the woods with an undercurrent of come-hither sweat. She would have been happy to stay beside him until the wedding—and the play about Winnie—had come and gone.

When he took his leave, however, his eyes didn't linger on her but on Nan, who said afterwards, "He wants to be recognizable. That's why he lost weight. If she ever shows up, he wants her to find him."

Lulu gave her a thoughtful look. "Maybe he found you instead."

4

ON MONDAY, THE wedding day, light breezes sent down spills and dustings of snow from treetops and rooftops. Lulu watched from the kitchen windows and thought of the sunderings and little falls in Winnie's mind. She was slipping on her coat when Nan's telephone rang and her heart went into spasm. The theatre? Had they tracked her down?

It was Blake wanting to speak to Jim.

She escaped outside. She would call Sal tomorrow. After all, Sal had encouraged her to take a full day or two off. And besides, she was from Montreal and actors from Montreal were notorious for not bothering to sign out. Tomorrow, she promised herself.

Nan had tapped twenty maples, hanging either one bucket or two, depending on the girth of the tree. She and Ducky were gathering up the sap, and Lulu lent a hand. They moved from tree to tree on the paths Nan had trod flat with her snowshoes, emptying the sap buckets into a big plastic pail, ferrying the pail on a toboggan down the slope, pouring the sap into the blue barrel beside the woodstove. The sap would keep until they could boil again later that night or in the morning.

Jim's voice called from the porch, "Phone!"

Jesus. A heart attack on repeat.

But the call was for Nan.

After lunch, Ducky went up the road to her father's, where she had left her wedding clothes. She would drive with Guy and Julie to the wedding, while Nan and Jim and Lulu would go earlier, delivering the precious cake to the community hall in Lanark.

Lulu asked Nan if she was nervous. They were sliding the tiered wedding cake into a carton open on three sides. The previous afternoon they had iced the layers with butter-cream icing and assembled them, then that morning Nan had decorated the base of each tier with green ribbon and poked white paper roses into the sides and top. The back-up cake, a single rectangular layer under tinfoil, was in its own box.

"Nervous? I'm just the mother of the groom. A minor role." Nan stopped and looked at Lulu. "You're worried about the play. I can do this. Go off and have some quiet time with your lines."

"I'm trying not to think about them." Lulu tapped her forehead. "Let my mind go blank and start over tomorrow."

"That helps?"

"I'm hoping so."

The wedding cake was a Bobak family recipe, the same pound cake Nan's mother-in-law had made when Nan married George Bobak. "Now I'm wondering if it's bad luck," Nan said. "I'll never forget George's aunt telling me on my wedding day that I had married an unlucky man." Her laugh was bleak. "It was one of the worst moments of my life."

"That wasn't the cake's fault," Lulu said.

"Thank you. Let's not be superstitious. I mean, you heard a banshee two nights ago and no one's dead yet."

A little before three o'clock, they set off in Nan's van. Jim was in the back between the two cartons of cake, a hand on each one to keep them steady. Lulu was up front wearing shoes rather than boots, expecting to be indoors or on cleared sidewalks. She hadn't bothered with a hat either, or gloves, or even her shoulder bag, and it made her feel like a girl again, shedding clothes at the end of winter.

It was the earliest Easter Monday in nearly a century, according to the car radio. Ten years ago, Lulu remembered, the great ice storm of 1998 bent every birch tree to the ground. Fifty years ago, give or take, the great fire in Lanark raged right up to her grandmother's door. Sixty-two years ago, she was born, in Seattle of all places, while a hundred years ago pioneers in the Ontario bush were working themselves to death. And what did that produce? Turning in her seat, "I met an Irish writer, a very rude and mischievous woman who joked that Canadians are Germans without the charm."

Nan and Jim laughed aloud. "She must have met our prime minister," Nan said.

Lulu rubbed the back of her neck and faced forward again. Sal had set her up with a massage therapist who had been better than nothing, but not good enough. Easter Monday. No performance until Wednesday night. She tried taking several deep breaths, then trained her eyes on the snow and the trees going by. Exit Lulu, she thought, pursued by a bear.

The road they were on—from Snow Road to Lanark's community hall and Baptist church—passed the long lane that led to the bride's farm.

Jim said from the back, "Your old enemy's farm."

"My mortal enemy," Nan agreed, and her hand went to her chest. In marrying the daughter of Janet Hepburn, Blake was allying himself with the childhood friend who had ditched Nan when she was eleven years old. A first jilting, like first love, lingers in the blood.

"Janet wanted to have the wedding at home," Nan said. "It's a big house, it's where Blake holds his church services, but Bethany wanted a real wedding in a real church. And Bethany is a match for her mother."

"And a match for Blake?" Lulu wondered.

"She's used to getting her way. She's the youngest."

Jim spoke again from the back, his voice firm in defending his brother. "She wouldn't be my choice, but she's Blake's choice."

"You know he spent four thousand dollars on an engagement ring?" Nan said. "She's even taking his name."

"She's traditional," Jim said. "I'm traditional myself in some ways."

"It's stupid," Nan said. A moment later, she smacked her forehead in disgust. "Oh, for God's sake." She had forgotten the notes for her speech. Well, she would just have to wing it; what else could she do?

A couple of hours earlier she had called Lulu into her bedroom, where she stood frowning in her bra and panties, her hair swept up in a bun secured by a pair of old-fashioned combs. Pointing to the two dark dresses laid out on the bed—"Which one, Lu?"

"Nan." Lulu had to stare. "You've got the oldest hairdo and the youngest body." A slender waist, no rolls of fat, great legs. She was reminded of Hazel, an elderly homeless woman she had taken pity on one Montreal blizzard, inviting her inside for a hot bath and a meal. Disrobed and in the bathtub, Hazel's body was as firm as a young woman's, which is what hauling a shopping cart all day and in all weathers had done for her.

"There'll be dancing," Nan said, "and I want to be comfortable." She slipped on one of the dresses.

"A DJ spinning records?"

"A local band." She turned and stood straight for Lulu.

"You look like a Mennonite," Lulu said. "Haven't you got a belt? . . . That's a little better." She stood back. "So fiddles and guitars."

"And Hugh Shapiro on the piano."

A tick of silence. "The piano tuner?"

Nan was looking down at herself. "You think I should have bought a new dress."

"And had your hair done."

The piano tuner. Lulu became aware of flecks of snow falling outside, changing the light in the room and everything it touched.

"I don't have the money," Nan said.

"If it were Jim's wedding, you would have bought a new dress."

Nan sank down on the bed and rubbed her bare arms. "He's lost so much weight. Have you noticed? I asked him, 'Is it happiness or unhappiness?' He said it's vegetarian food. He's been cooking for a friend who's a vegetarian."

"He's in love," Lulu said.

The day before, passing behind him in the kitchen as he opened his laptop, Lulu had glimpsed the young woman filling his screen, a tiny-boned face framed by a wealth of hair. Intending to elicit a smile: "Jim, you'll never forget her that way." And he had flinched in pain.

"Is it serious?" Touching his shoulder.

"Not anymore."

"Who ended it?"

"I ended it."

"Then get rid of her picture," she said, sitting down beside him.

They were alone and something in him must have given way, for he proceeded to tell her about the woman in the picture, the vegetarian he had been cooking for—Maya—who was older than he was, more experienced, and she had already moved on to another relationship, while he woke up every morning from long, involved dreams about her. He felt lost, left behind. He had no idea where his life was going.

"Well, try to resist going back for more. I've done that too often."

"Lu?" He paused. "Do you remember when you read my palm?"

She nodded. She remembered all too well that summer day a dozen years ago, the two of them cycling to Guy's sugar bush, her ugly confrontation with her brother, then afterwards sharing an orange and reading Jim's palm in fun, but going cold when she saw how short his lifeline was.

He said, "What did you see that you wouldn't tell me? You were reading my palm and you stopped."

Lulu felt her lips form an awkward smile. "I stopped because I didn't know what I was talking about, that's the reason I stopped."

"Maya read my palm."

Lulu looked at him hard. "What did *she* see?"

"She says I'll be dead before my next birthday."

"Oh, Jim. She's messing with you. Anyone who told you that doesn't know you or love you."

He sat there, working his thumb into his palm.

"Is she at university with you? Doing a master's in music too?"

He shook his head. She was at Harvard. Doing a doctorate in neuroscience.

"Okay. That's impressive."

"She *is* impressive. She's very ambitious." He said, "We met at a concert."

Lulu's heart went out to him. She imagined high-flying Maya intent on gain and glory. A mere musicology student like Jim wouldn't cut it. "You're twenty-three?" she said.

"Twenty-four in September."

"What else did she do to you?" Lulu wanted to know.

There was a long pause before Jim answered. "I guess she abused my love," he said. "I didn't start out wanting to be appreciated for all I did for her, but after a while it got to me. I just felt very tired."

"In love? I didn't know." Nan stopped rubbing her arms. "He talks to you. I'm so glad."

Lulu sank down beside her on the bed. "I'm jealous of you, darling."

"Whatever for? You look wonderful. Like a ripe plum." Nan reached over and fingered the purple silkiness of Lulu's dress and admired the collar of four strands of pearls, which Lulu maintained kept her neck warmer than a scarf.

Lulu said, "I wish I had a child."

Nan stared. "You've never mentioned wanting children."

It was seeing Tony Lloyd again, it was having the lake bottom of her past dredged up. "I'm as surprised as you are," Lulu said. "I guess I'm finding out."

Approaching Lanark now, Jim began to talk about how much he loved *Madame Bovary*. Doomed marriages must have been in the air. He had never read anything like it, he said. And yet he had. Other books tried to do the same thing. But *Madame Bovary* was fresh. It was simple, precise, evocative. He liked how short it was too.

Listening to him, Lulu remembered the boy who had always had his nose deep in a book. A reader and a dreamer.

"It's so romantically charged," he went on. "At the end, when Justin's crying on her grave, there's that line that would be ridiculous in any other book: 'His immense regret sweet as the moon and fathomless as the night.'"

His mother found him in the rear-view mirror and said, "You've still got your great memory." Her face had softened. The nervous worry was gone.

They were coming into Lanark itself now, passing houses in wooded lots set back off the curving road. The sky was heavy with end-of-winter clouds, low on the horizon, dark mauve, deep pink. The rosy tint on the fluffy snowbanks reminded Lulu of her beloved pudding-faced grandmother buried in the cemetery on the far side of town. Louise Irene Blake, after whom she and Ducky had both been named. She wondered how happy Ducky was at still being called Ducky now that she was seventeen. She should ask her. Maybe she was more than ready to be Irene.

5

FROM HER PEW Lulu turned to watch the procession enter the church: young men in black suits and young women in next to nothing. Four shivering bridesmaids teetered past on stiletto heels, while the men strolled in, warm and comfortable. The sight made her want to riot. Fifteen minutes passed and no bride. Then in she came on her father's arm, a big brunette in a froth of white, beaming and weeping. Blake's face closed like a door as she came down the aisle.

This was going to be worth watching. A wedding of people who disliked each other and from now on would have to see more of each other. On one side, a family of evangelical and prolific farm folk. On the other, ex–New Yorkers with deep roots in Canada and their own idiosyncratic ways.

Lulu had spotted Tony Lloyd in a pew across the aisle. His ample companion was recognizably Roseanne, Janet's sister. And that must be the mother of the bride, Janet herself, whose huge fallen bosom rolled around behind a pink-satin blouse. Not a trace remained of the willowy schoolgirl who had turned the air blue on the basketball court, knocking Lulu and Nan, and every other hapless player, out of her path, until at nineteen she made her shock marriage to Eric, the born-again farm boy, and became born-again herself.

The bride was also nineteen and on a similar headlong rush through life, even if at present she was dripping tears into her bouquet of white roses. Jim slipped a tissue into her hand and she mopped her eyes, while Lulu in her pew pondered the terrible choices we make in life.

Wouldn't it be grand, she thought, if one of them, bride or groom, turned tail right now and made for parts unknown. But who has the courage to make a public run for it? To stand up in the middle of a performance and say, "I can't do this." Gripping the pew in front of her, she steadied her own surge of panic by focusing on the mismatched couple trapped like rats. There, through the cascade of chiffon, was Bethany's widening midriff if you knew to look or if you made an educated guess, and there was Blake holding himself away from her as if he were his own ten-foot pole.

Blake's inaudible mumble. Bethany's cracking, emotional voice. The elderly Baptist preacher's cheery zeal on their behalf.

Then it was over and they were all making their way by car to the reception at the community hall on the northeast edge of town. Inside the hall, Lulu caught up with Tony, who was wreathed in silly smiles as Roseanne steered him around.

Grabbing Lulu's arm, he drew her to one side and opened his hand on a brown mini-envelope.

The sleeping pills. "Awesome," she said, tucking his offering inside her bra.

And he bustled back to Roseanne.

Gazing around her, Lulu took in the age-old malady of young women trying too hard. Bare shoulders, steep necklines, fixed smiles. Tattoos—now that was 2008. These were small-town people, she thought, her glance embracing the whole crowd. Mostly overweight, overdressed, overfriendly, and white. She assumed some of the guests were connected to Blake's life as a pastor, others to his day job as a schoolteacher, and she tried to figure out who was who. She had learned that the three groomsmen were not friends of his but Bethany's brothers. Perhaps Blake was a man with a following but no good friends. And perhaps not much of a following either.

Jim came by, making sure she was all right, which was when she learned that no drink was to be had. Of course. Evangelicals. It was to be a dry wedding.

Except for the tears. Poor Nan's flowed down her face.

First, her microphone let out a shriek and she jumped back, then she apologized for forgetting her notes, then thanked everyone for coming. Then stood for a moment frowning and collecting herself. Janet's speech, which had preceded Nan's, had suffered from no such hesitation. The mother of the bride, robust and not to be gainsaid, had welcomed everyone into a circle of love and thanked the Lord for uniting their own inspired pastor with their youngest daughter. "The greatest description of marriage," she said, "is in Ephesians 5. 'Wives, submit to your husbands as to the Lord.' That's verse 22." A weighty pause. "However, let's not forget verse 25. 'Husbands, love your wives as Christ loved the Church.' But why am I telling you what you already know?" Janet's voice rose in a full-throated trill. "We take you both into our hearts, full of gladness that you are marrying in the Lord." Scattered "amens" floated up from various parts of the hall.

Nan, on the other hand, was remembering the groom as a small boy so talented in drawing he would whip off sketches in minutes flat. "Here." And he would hand her a picture of the pigeons living on their windowsill in Manhattan, or of a praying mantis accurate in every detail. "He loved to dress up. He loved to clomp around in his grandmother's cast-off high heels. I thought he might become an artist or an actor. Then he got into model cars and airplanes, and I thought, engineer, architect, dentist. It never occurred to me he would turn into a holy man. But mothers are the last ones to understand their children, or so it seems. And now he's starting his own family." She paused, glancing over at Blake with a nervous smile. The flash of anger in his face stopped her.

Just us. His cautionary words from the other night: no one else knew Bethany was pregnant. She must have remembered, because her words dried up.

"He and Bethany—Blake and Bethany," she stammered, "will make their lives together now—and all we want is their happiness." Her face crumpled on the word "happiness." She put her hand over her eyes.

"Breathe," called out Guy, when her shoulders began to shake.

"Love is hard," she finally gasped out. "So help each other."

Lulu, from her table towards the back, saw the groom head for the side exit. Saw him plunge outside into the snow. Saw Jim follow him and after a moment she followed too. Blake was swearing as he struggled to light a cigarette; Jim was telling him to take it easy, "Mom didn't make you look bad." But Blake was having none of it. "She can't even buy a dress?" he railed. "She thinks it's a funeral?"

Lulu had to smile. She had seen directors this enraged, blaming the actors for everything. And why? Because they were ashamed to death of the play they had directed.

Putting her hand on Blake's arm, she was startled by the blast of heat pouring out through his jacket sleeve. His body was steaming. "Anyway, her dress isn't what's bothering you," she said. "Let's have one of those." She tapped the package of cigarettes in his breast pocket. "And the matches," she said.

Jim ran the back of his hand across his lips. "Let's go in. People are wondering."

"Tell them I'm having a smoke." Blake was actually grinding his teeth and Lulu thought, What a way to start a marriage.

"A stroke?" Jim said.

"Jim," Lulu said, "go in and keep your mother company." He gave her a grateful look and left her alone with Blake.

Then she and Blake were smoking amid the snowbanks. Ice crystals formed on his shoulders and on the top of his head. A runaway groom, tapping cigarette ash into the snow.

"Why are you so mean to your mother?" Lulu said.

Blake, sullen and unreachable, drew on his cigarette.

"She's not the problem and you know it."

Several snowflakes landed on his jacket sleeve, lingered a moment, and melted. Turning her head, she saw snow falling softly on the cars in the parking lot and on the fields beyond. She said, "I half expected you to bolt before the vows."

He looked up. "Is that what you would have done?"

"Probably not." She stubbed out her cigarette with her shoe. "But marriage is a risk I've never wanted to take."

He smoked in silence, then seemed to come out of himself. "You must be cold." And he slipped off his jacket and draped it over her shoulders.

"Thank you."

Surprised and touched by his thoughtfulness. Inside his welcome body heat, she smelled spicy deodorant and not-unpleasant sweat, plus something metallic that she recognized from costumes hung up to air after a performance. Fear. Adrenalin. And her own panic surged back. She closed her eyes against a wave of despair.

"Why not?" Blake said.

She opened her eyes and stared at him.

"Why is marriage a risk you never wanted to take?"

"Oh." She made a face. "Afraid of being trapped, I think."

The snow was falling gently, landing on his dark hair, his white shirt. Movement come to rest, she thought. "You're having second thoughts," she said. "It's natural. Likely most people do."

She knew only part of the story. That Blake—to all appearances alienated from his mother—had nevertheless been drawn to Nan's part of the world ten years earlier, moving from Philadelphia to Lanark to found an evangelical church. Whether he realized it or not, he must have wanted to be front and centre in his mother's life. A reminder. A reproach. In Lanark he had discovered in Janet's family his key adherents: Janet and Eric and their five children, the youngest of whom had just made an unwilling husband of him at the age of thirty-two. Six weeks ago had come the sudden announcement. *Mr. and Mrs. Eric Taylor request your presence as their daughter Bethany Ruth joins her hand in Holy Matrimony to Blake Rufus Sharpe, son of Mrs. Nancy Catherine Waterman of Snow Road Station and Mr. John Cecil Sharpe of Chicago.*

Obviously, no mention of the paternal complication.

Lulu knew from Nan that when she had finally owned up, it was first and most unhappily to Blake himself. "You're telling me I'm Blake Blake?" he had said. "What are you? Agatha Christie planting clues?"

So not without a savage sense of humour.

"Don't you think it's time?" she said now, giving him back his jacket.

"Time?"

"To face the music," she said.

6

INSIDE THE HALL he veered off to the washroom, while she went over to the head table where Jim and Ducky were sitting with Nan, whose trembling hands had given up trying to raise her water glass to her lips.

"He's fine," Lulu reassured them. "He's just gone to the washroom."

She still felt the body heat from his jacket, still felt surprised.

An older man—not old, but older, in his sixties like herself—was leaning against the near wall and she caught him looking in her direction. She held his gaze a moment, then turned away. Tall and lean, stylish in black, a bony face and a hatchet of grey hair—he reminded her of Samuel Beckett. She shot him another look and found him still staring at her. Where did you come from? she thought. Not from around here.

A pair of bridesmaids shivered nearby. Eyeing their near-nakedness, she turned to Jim and said with scant sympathy, "They must think they look cool."

Jim's glance followed hers and he said, "Sometimes coolness—looking cool—is just distress."

Lulu rested her eyes on his thoughtful, tired, humane face. "You're way ahead of me, Jim."

Now, looking around her with Jim's eyes, she saw a sea of distress. Roly-poly Tony Lloyd swaddled in worry and failure; young women dressed like guttering candles of self-conscious agony; in-laws in pain; and everyone else hearty and on edge. A dry wedding in a sea of distress.

Bethany was off in a corner with another bridesmaid. Feeling sorry for her as well as curious, Lulu went over to speak to her.

"I've got something in my eyes," the bride laughed. "It's crazy." She was still dabbing with Jim's tissue.

"She's allergic to something," her friend said.

"Marriage," Lulu said. "I don't blame you. Maybe eye drops?"

"We've tried."

"I'm fine," Bethany said. "I'm better."

"So when was the first time you set eyes on Blake?" Lulu asked.

"At home." Bethany laughed again. "He was playing his guitar in our living room, leading hymns. I refused to come downstairs. I was sick of all that."

"I didn't know he played guitar."

"He has an amazing voice too. That's what made me come downstairs. I was nine years old."

"He made quite an impression," Lulu said.

"I told myself, 'I'm going to marry that man.'"

And Bethany's eyes swung to the spot across the room where that man had reappeared at last. They watched him go to his mother and kiss her on the forehead. Saw Nan nod in Bethany's direction and now Blake was coming over to them, seeking out his relieved young bride, whose romantic precociousness had Lulu remembering a conversation the previous summer, three teenage girls on a dock as she paddled by. "My favourite meal is spaghetti, peas, and salad," one said.

"I want to be married so badly," another said. "Not now. But one day."

"I won't eat oatmeal," the third said. "I won't eat jam, Brussels sprouts, cucumbers, or olives. I won't eat cow."

And then they were out of hearing, three girls staking out their lonely appetites.

No danger of Brussels sprouts on the banquet table overseen by a handful of church women, but there was indeed cow. Lulu surveyed the meatballs and barbecued ribs, the macaroni and cheese, the great bowls of coleslaw and green salad. Nan joined her. They filled their plates and were carrying them to a table off to one side when Janet swooped down, all flap and gush and iron will. "We adore Blake," she said to Nan. "He's one of us. And now you'll *have* to have tea with me." Taking charge of Nan's plate and Nan, she steered her back to the head table.

Lulu sat down beside her brother. "How is your neck?"

"A hundred percent," Guy said.

"The acupuncture?"

"No. Clearing up some lady trouble. I stuck my neck too far out and now I've pulled it back in."

Her irresistible brother was running true to form. She asked him if Julie (who was out of hearing on the other side of the round table) knew about this lady trouble of his. "Most certainly not," her brother said. And if she found out? "I would lie," he said. "I would lie and lie until I could lie no more. Then I would get down on my knees and apologize abjectly."

"My brother the heartbreaker." Rolling her eyes.

A big, raw-boned woman with false teeth appeared out of nowhere and plunged across the table at them. "You're so good-looking!" she declared. And Guy readily agreed. "She is. Lulu looks great."

"*You*," the woman said.

Guy threw up his hands. "Me?" He grimaced with delighted embarrassment and Lulu ran her eyes over her silver-haired brother. He spent his life in the open air, that's why. A winter tan takes ten years off a person's age. "Who was *that*?" she said, thinking the church ladies must be imbibing on the sly.

"There are fifty widows in this town. I can't be expected to remember them all. Tell me you're not the same," he grinned back at her. "You and I have never had to do without. That's why we're so close."

He caught her startled reaction. "Don't tell me I'm wrong," he said.

Lulu took a moment to answer, thrown back into the quarrels of the past when Guy could be as cold and contemptuous to her as Blake was to Nan. A lot of embattled history led up to their present truce. Encounters that were like acid baths, when he greeted her by saying What do *you* want? Or when he wondered how a two-bit drunk didn't stumble off the stage. They had been taking turns looking after their sick and dying mother, and he'd come upon Lulu taking out the garbage and stooped to pick up the gin bottles that got loose, not saying a word until they were back inside. Then that devastating question. No one had known how to hurt her more.

"When it counts," she said finally. They were close when it counted.

The tall stranger—the one who kept looking at her—was standing with Blake, every so often making an aside that drew the other's attention. She said to her brother, "Who's that leaning against the wall?"

"No clue."

"Is it John Sharpe?"

"Nan's ex? It might be."

"The grim ghost at the wedding. The ghost of things to come." With a rueful laugh.

"Hey," her brother said, reading her troubled face. "We thought you were terrific, all of us did."

"Did you? Why? I know you told me before, but tell me again." Still moved and gratified that he and Julie and Nan had driven to Ottawa for opening night.

"You kept me awake," her brother said. "I didn't nod off once. I couldn't take my eyes off you. You made me laugh. And at the end you broke my heart."

Tears sprang into her eyes and Guy put his arm around her. "You're a champ," he said.

7

DINNER WAS OVER. Jim was dancing with his mother, who was more graceful on the dance floor than Lulu would have predicted. She had never before pictured her old friend as light on her feet, as a rival in any form, and a jaded voice in the back of her head said, That's why your friendship has lasted.

A few feet away from where she sat with Guy, a stooped and white-haired gent whistled under his breath, his craggy, running-to-seed face taking in all the wedding guests with a benign regard. "May I sit here?" he said, turning and parking himself cautiously on the chair beside her. "If I behave myself." He reached into his pocket and out fell a filthy comb. Lulu retrieved it from the floor and he thanked her, then proceeded to run it through his head of white hair and joke about how he was falling apart.

"Not your hair," she said to him. "It's magnificent."

"Balding men hate me for it," he said.

He was like the shabby old men Beckett was so fond of. Returned once more and against her will to the play and the dreaded performances to come. It seemed every wedding distraction led to the same knot in her guts. In preparing for the part, she had discovered that Beckett's wife was an austere Frenchwoman six years older than himself. He had married a version of his mother, but only—this amused Lulu—after the younger Englishwoman he was rather passionately involved with informed him she was moving to Paris to be with him, and he needed to dampen her ardour. It was no secret how attractive Beckett was to women.

And there was Hugh Shapiro at the piano, sleeves rolled up, hands, wrists, lower arms on fetching display roving over the keyboard. The band had set themselves up on a makeshift stage on the far side of the hall, and Hugh shared an easy rapport with the fiddle player and the two guys on guitar.

Others crowded the dance floor. A pair of bridesmaids in bare feet. Tony Lloyd and Roseanne floating by like oversized dumplings. Guy's wife, Julie, propelled by a paunchy fellow in a tweed jacket. For Julie loved to dance and Guy did not. Never had. His eyes didn't leave the dance floor, however. "Nan's the one who got away," he said to Lulu.

"Well, I doubt Nan would put it that way." Their summer romance all those years ago still coloured her brother's life, but that was nothing to how it had complicated Nan's, causing her to throw in her lot with the wrong man. John Sharpe. Who had to be the stranger with whom Blake was at ease, the one who kept running her up and down with his eyes. Nan had never talked much about her failed first marriage, except to say it was a terrible mistake, the first of two, the one leading to the other, out of the frying pan of an alpha male and into the ashes of passive-aggressive George. I don't want to talk about it, she would say when Lulu would probe this part of her past; I don't, I can't, it's too shameful. And Lulu let her be. She had her own wounds and reservoirs of shame that she kept to herself.

But seeing the alpha male in the flesh now gave her curiosity a second wind. How had her old friend gone from this forceful man to someone as boring as George? Maybe that was Nan: playing it safe, settling for too little.

"Nan was the one," Guy repeated. "She's not like anyone else. She's the most independent woman I know. But quiet about it."

"You admire that."

"I love it," he said. "She knows how to leave a person alone."

"And Julie doesn't?"

Her brother spread his hands and shrugged.

"Do you remember Tony Lloyd?" she said.

"Your old flame?"

"He's dancing with Roseanne."

"Get out," Guy said. "He looks like Santa Claus with a hangover."

"Can you believe it? I have to assume I've changed as drastically as he has."

"You haven't," Guy said.

"You don't think I've aged?"

"Lu." Her brother gave her a look of disbelief. "We've *all* aged."

And Lulu threw back her head and guffawed at her own atrocious vanity. "Oh, Guy," she said. "We'll be dead soon."

"Well, here's to life." Filling their glasses from the water pitcher on the table. "If only I'd known, I would have packed my flask." He clicked his glass against hers, and she teased him about the tipsy church lady who would be more than happy to share.

The band was playing "Moon River" and Lulu gave herself up to the song. It wasn't fair, she thought. A man playing "Moon River" had the same overwhelming advantage as a soccer player with beautiful thighs.

"What about the piano player?" she said. "Do you know him?"

Guy cocked his right eyebrow at her. "Not you too."

"What?"

"Let me just say we must have the best-tuned piano in the county."

"You have competition," Lulu smiled. "Who is he when he's not tuning pianos or playing them?"

"A mediocre painter."

She let that sink in without comment. Meanwhile, formidable Janet, with Bethany in tow, corralled the bridegroom and forced him onto the dance floor with his bride.

"So what's it like," she said dryly, "watching your son get married?"

"Strange," Guy said. "He's my son and I barely know him."

"And whose fault is that?"

"It must be mine. I've tried. I guess I haven't tried hard enough. I'm just an old reprobate in his eyes. An embarrassment."

"I'm sorry," Lulu said, and she was. Her brother had always wanted a son and he was an excellent father, he and Ducky were devoted to each other, so it seemed the worst kind of joke that his son-at-last wanted nothing to do with him.

"How long do you give them?" Guy said.

"Three years? We're looking at a very unhappy man."

A year ago she had been in a museum in Montreal, going from room to room, getting wearier by the minute, until she entered a gallery with a life-sized sculpture in the middle, and it was like falling in love across a crowded room. She walked right up to it. Degas's *Little Dancer Aged Fourteen*. Everything else fell away—the visitors, the paintings on the walls, the guide with her entourage going by.

The little dancer was wearing a tutu, her head held high, her arms and hands behind her back, her foot far forward and turned out at an angle. She was so young and pretty and poor and hard-working, and so unprotected. More alive than all the living people around her. Lulu stood looking for a long time, not tired anymore.

In another room, on another floor, something else claimed her: a huge tableau of neo-Nazi skinheads filling the wall with homoerotic desire. Standing in front of it, mesmerized, was Blake.

He didn't notice her. He didn't notice anyone.

That's all. Enough to make her think she had glimpsed his inner self and understood.

She saw him again an hour later sitting outside on one of the plinth-like benches, and she hesitated, he was so lost in thought. She was about to pass him by when he looked up.

"I was in the museum," he said, turning and pointing his chin at the low-slung concrete building.

"I saw you. You were absorbed. Transfixed. I didn't want to disturb you."

He coloured and looked down at the sidewalk—a few stray leaves from a small city tree, a few cigarette butts. She recalled her own rapt scrutiny of the little dancer and out of fairness modified her thought: how you look at a piece of art tells you more about the power of the art than anything else: its power to locate the emotion deep inside you.

"He's not afraid," she said to him. "Attila Lukacs. That's what I admired. To paint what he desires. He's shameless about what he wants. I couldn't tear my eyes away either."

Blake straightened his back.

"But that's an artist's job," she said. "Not being afraid. Are you in Montreal for a while?"

"Until tomorrow," Blake said. Then added, "I'm here for meetings." In case she might have any notion they would see more of each other.

She felt his awkward reserve and her own unimportance, and didn't know what else to say. They parted, he walking in one direction and she in the other.

How alive their history was. You escape for a while. You think you've escaped forever. But here's Janet Hepburn burning out the centre of Nan's life yet again. Here's Blake, the unintended result of an early affair. And Jim, taking a moment to stand off to the side and be alone with his heartache.

And now here was her brother going over to Blake, reaching out his hand, making an effort to congratulate him. Blake shook the extended hand, nodded, turned away. And Guy was left to look and feel foolish. He caught Lulu's eye and shrugged. Uphill battles, thought Lulu. This was another one.

People were still dancing. The wedding cake had yet to be cut. And Lulu felt a pair of hands on her shoulders—here was the father of the child she had decided not to have asking her to dance.

8

"THIS IS MORE like it," Tony said, guiding her across the floor. A hand firmly on her back, his beard tickling the side of her face, his voice in her ear.

It was like dancing with a soft mattress, and indeed she would not have minded lying down. "I thought the Mounties would be on to you by now," she said, and enjoyed the rich laugh that tumbled out of his belly.

"So who's this client of yours in Montreal?" she said.

"Three guesses," he replied. Her fat and cagey gold smuggler.

"A drug dealer."

"Classier than that."

"Classier. The Italian mafia? They're big in Montreal."

No. He knew them, but he didn't deal with them, not directly.

"Let me think," she said.

Dancing with Tony reminded her of her great-uncle who had steered her across the floor a few times when she was a girl, his footwork as assured as a snowplough clearing a winter road. There used to be dance halls all over this part of the world; even Snow Road Station had one in a converted warehouse down by the tracks.

"I give up. Tell me."

"The son of a powerful politician in Bangkok. A spoilt brat. He goes to McGill."

"No kidding. You take his son the gold—"

"And the son does the rest."

"You know, I've been trying to picture how you carry gold bricks on your person."

"Lu," he said, "bullion, not bricks. They're like biscuits, they weigh an ounce. You can slip them into your shoes or into your underwear."

"You don't wear underwear."

He chuckled. "You remember."

The song ended and he enveloped her in one of his giant hugs before walking her back to the table. There he touched her arm and said, "I used to believe in the good in people too." He indicated all the naive, churchgoing folk around them. "But I've seen a lot. I've seen how bad people really are."

Lulu took his measure. "Darling," she said, "that's no excuse."

"My ex doesn't age," Nan said to her. She was twisting her wedding band around her finger. "He looks the same as ever."

"Where *is* he?"

"Over there, talking to your Tony."

Ah. She had guessed right. Tony was deep in conversation with the lean man in black, John Sharpe.

Nan's fingers went to the shiny scar in the middle of her forehead. A pained habit of long standing.

"Bad memories?" Lulu said.

A little shake of Nan's head.

"What, then?" Lulu reached for Nan's hand and drew it away from worrying her forehead.

"Nothing really." Nan managed a smile. "I'm all right."

"You're sure?"

"I am, dear Lulu."

Lulu's roaming eyes came to rest once again on Hugh Shapiro. Turning back to Nan, "There's your admirer."

The song was over. Hugh was standing up. The band was taking a break.

Nan snorted. "He called me bony."

"Boys do that," Lulu said. "They wash your face in snow if they like you, or take your hat and wear it home."

"I remind him of his old girlfriend, that's all. He's confusing me with somebody else."

"Oh, I think he's drawn to you."

"Stop it, Lu. You're the one who's smitten."

"Totally." Lulu leant forward with frank enthusiasm.

As if their conversation had summoned him, her limping, fetching man came over to their table. "I won't sit down," acknowledging Lulu's welcoming gesture, "I just wanted to say love *is* hard. Nobody gets it right."

"That was terrible." Nan dropped her face into her hands. "It's a wedding. I should have called them the adorable couple. I should have had my hair done."

"Your hair is as it should be," Hugh said.

Such simple words, Lulu thought, but what other man would have said them?

Then she was being offered a slice of wedding cake by the ex-husband, who had a plate in either hand. "You're John Sharpe," she said, giving him a cool, assessing look. She had been on her way back from the washroom when he intercepted her. The music was over. The band was packing up.

"And you're Tony's Lulu."

"I'm my own Lulu," she said. "And don't you forget it."

He smiled slightly and they stood without speaking, eating the excellent pound cake. He asks me nothing, she thought, but he doesn't move away. "It's a family recipe," she said, and took pleasure in adding that it came from Nan's *second* husband. "What's your verdict?"

"Passable."

She smiled. He was the sort of taciturn man she had a knack for because non-answers didn't throw her and moodiness did not intimidate her.

Nan came over to them, wanting her to know that she and Jim were leaving now, heading home to make sure the sap buckets weren't overflowing. Did she want to come with them, or would she stay on and get a ride with someone else? Lulu hesitated. She had been toying with the idea of asking Hugh Shapiro to take her home.

Sharpe said, "I could drive you."

"You've got a car?" Nan said to him.

"I rented it at the airport."

"But it's out of your way," Nan said. "Aren't you staying in town with Blake?"

"It can't be that far. This isn't Chicago."

"Or Guy could bring you." Nan turned to Lulu. "Unless he's gone already. Why don't you come with us?"

Her ex said, "What's the matter? Are you afraid we're going to talk about you?"

Nan winced and looked away.

9

HUGH SHAPIRO HAD already left when Lulu went looking for him, and she couldn't find her brother, so she had fallen back on John Sharpe after all, and now he was bantering with her about directions. He preferred bigger roads to the twisty back way, which meant heading to Snow Road Station via the town of Perth, a longer route with the added bonus of more time in her company. He hoped she was amenable.

His SUV was higher off the ground and roomier than she was used to. For a while the nearly-full moon kept them company and Lulu recalled the stray pup that became Jim's dog Moon hightailing it up the lane to Nan's on just such a moonlit night—escaping a pack of wolves—and how that thrilling rescue was eclipsed later on when an injured Moon didn't make it home.

"The back of beyond," Sharpe muttered of the world they were driving through.

"Lanark used to be livelier," she said in its defence, "especially before the fire. It was the prettiest village. It had everything you could want."

And she was back under the deep shade of century-old maples, walking past the hardware store, the tinsmith, the barber shop, the five-and-dime, the fire hall and the town hall, the dance hall and hotel, the florist's and the hairdresser's. It was a world unto itself, a coherent world you could hold in your mind's eye. Then in a single hot and windy afternoon in June the coherence went up in smoke. A hundred homes and dozens of livelihoods disappeared. In the chaos that followed, cheap buildings got thrown up any-which-way and the eyesores remained to this day.

She said, "Now I guess it's a dying town."

"Oh, it's *dead*." He let out a short bark of a laugh and she laughed a little too.

"Didn't you meet Nan in Toronto?" she said, directing her gaze at his beaky profile.

"Correct." He was in Toronto for business a lot back then, and Nan had stopped him for directions and then refused to follow them. He had come upon her later, still lost.

Lulu said, "I didn't know her then. We'd lost touch. There was a long spell when we didn't see each other."

Twenty-five years, terra incognita. Only when she had learned about Nan's brother's death, learned that Nan had taken over his house at the lake, learned that they were both at the lake at the same time, did she seek her out and resurrect a friendship that meant the world to her when she was a girl.

"She told me you were together for six years," Lulu said.

"It felt like a hundred," Sharpe said.

"Romantic guy. No wonder she left you."

"She *trapped* me." He turned his head and held her gaze. "Like Bethany's done to Blake." He turned his eyes back to the road. "Let's not pretend that marriage is what he wants."

"You and Blake seem close," she said after a while.

They were. Blake had stayed with him every summer after the divorce. "I mothered Blake more than Nan did."

"I've heard this line before," Lulu said wearily. "Men are the new mothers and women are selfish and full of themselves."

"Believe me. Sometimes it's true."

They were approaching Snow Road on the 509 and it was snowing again. The air was reasserting itself and Lulu said, "I've known Nan since I was fourteen. She's a fine person and a fine mother. She cares a lot about your Blake."

"As it turns out, he's not *my* Blake. Aren't you his aunt?"

Lulu couldn't get used to it, but she was. She was his aunt and he was her nephew, although the knowledge of their connection had come very late in the day. He remained for her Nan's troubled and distant son who resisted sympathy, who was loyal to the wrong parent, who didn't seem to give a damn about his real father. And yet there was their recent moment in the falling snow, his jacket over her shoulders, his pensiveness and a certain openness. He seemed more real to her now. As did this ex-husband.

"Let's start again," Sharpe said. "Talk to me about yourself."

But she didn't feel like talking about herself. "You first. What do you do in Chicago?"

He was a wealth manager for a private equity firm and he named the firm, but it meant nothing to Lulu.

So you're rich, she thought. "Are you good at it?"

"I am. I've made a lot of money. I could do the same for you."

"Oh, honey. No, you couldn't. I'm broke."

"Borrow some money from your brother and I'll invest it for you. I'm serious. What have you got to lose?"

"Guy's money," she said. "But maybe you wouldn't mind that."

"I could be your lucky break, if you let me."

"My ticket to heaven?" she smiled.

"Why not?" Giving her a swift appraising look.

He slowed down to the speed limit and slowed down even more as the road curved towards the river. Before reaching the bridge, he pulled over and turned off the engine. The headlights died.

"I don't know about you," he said, "but my tongue is hanging out. If you poke around in the glove compartment, you'll find a mickey of gin."

"Ah." And soon she was cradling it in her hands—dear old Bombay Sapphire. Dry weddings should be outlawed, they agreed, they were crimes against humanity.

"No tumblers," he said. "Sorry. We'll have to make do."

Lulu unscrewed the bottle, and they passed it back and forth in the dark quiet of the car. She remembered a summer's night on Cape Cod, drinking martinis so delicious she had asked the bartender what proportions he used. "Proportions?" he'd said. "I mean, how much vermouth?" "Vermouth," he'd said, "what vermouth?"

Straight gin. She put her head back and let it do its wonderful work.

"Lulu Blake." His voice turned over her name. "Where does Lulu come from?"

She told him, hearing herself sound as relaxed and tired as she felt.

"Louise," he repeated. "Louise Blake. But you prefer Lulu. Racy women get called Lulu."

"Tell that to my grandmother," she said.

"Bad girls," he went on. "Bad girls get called Lulu."

"I am bad. A bad old girl."

"I know. I watched you."

She smiled. "And what did you see?"

"You didn't belong at that wedding."

"Is that so. Why not?"

"You're warm and open, unlike that frozen crew of stuffed shirts and old biddies."

"Come on. They're not all stuffed shirts."

"Well, they're not like you."

She laughed, not displeased. He passed her the bottle, she took another sip and passed it back.

"You're an outsider like me." He reached across and slid his fingers inside the cuff of her coat, stroking the underside of her wrist. "We have a lot in common, we could have a good time together."

"Could we?"

"You know we could."

"It's late," she said, moving her arm away.

"I'm not going anywhere."

"I am. You're taking me home."

He stroked the side of her face, the side of her head.

"I mean it," she said, turning her face away.

"What's the matter?" His tone changed. "I thought you liked men."

"Oh, for Christ's sake," she said.

"Don't get mad, sweetheart." He pushed his fingers through her hair, not gently. "We'll go in a while. After we've had some fun."

"Not with me." Pulling away again.

"Very much with you."

He jerked her back by the hair, hard, and Lulu cried out. "Come on," he said, "you like this. Show me you're still hot."

She pushed him away. "Go fuck yourself."

But he grabbed her wrist and twisted it, and in a fury she sank her teeth into his hand and didn't let go. That made for a satisfying yelp.

"*Cunt*." He smacked her with his free hand and shoved her against the door.

And then she was standing on the shoulder. He had driven off.

Un-fucking-believable. Now what? The taste of his hand fouled her mouth and she spat.

Well, she would walk. From here it was a quarter mile or so to the white church, where she would turn right and carry on to the turnoff to the lake road and Nan's. Maybe four miles in all. She was wearing low-heeled pumps. No hat or gloves. It was about eleven at night.

She looked up at the sky. No moon now, and not a star to be seen. All of them done in by low clouds gently shedding snow. But quiet. It smelled of winter.

Then she heard him coming back, saw the wide sweep of headlights on the bridge, and instinctively she crouched low in the shallow ditch.

He slowed down, looking for her.

She made herself smaller, dropping onto her knees, turning on her side, head down, facing away from the road. The outer rim of his headlights picked out the birch trees just beyond. She heard his car pull over on the far shoulder and squeezed her eyes shut.

The slam of the car door and fear opened her groin. So this is how it works. Our bodies give us away. Not sexual excitement, but the wet arousal of fear.

She heard his feet crunching on the snow and ice, and lay still. An old actor's voice in her head. "If you can't defend yourself, you can't defend the character." Telling her to stand up for herself against a bastard director. She had, and that bastard had fired her.

The footsteps stopped. He had found her.

Nothing happened for a long moment and then she became aware of sudden heat on her back, the wet heaviness, the homeless stink. He was peeing on her. Through her shock she remembered Dougie Lumley peeing on her when she was four years old. The boyish wielding of his wee dick and his gargantuan glee. She remembered the yellow dress she was wearing and how she was sitting—two steps down on the small front porch—her back to him—and the summer day that got momentarily sunnier and inexplicably hotter, like a magnifying glass trained on her back—while above her Dougie laughed his head off.

She didn't move. Not until the sound of his car faded into the distance and disappeared. When she got to her feet, it was like standing up in a small boat. She lurched and caught herself.

10

SNOW ROAD LAY ahead of her—the river, the bridge, what was left of a village that was still itself, but no longer itself. Winnie's words came to her like perfect eggs "To have been always what I am—and so changed from what I was."

Snow was coming down. She could count the flakes.

She started to walk. She had space. She had the use of her legs. And at last she had Winnie loud and clear in her head. Peed on, that's all. Not run over or sliced open or roasted on a spit. Another heavenly night.

She was on the bridge and then across it. Here was where the freight trains used to run and here was she, a hobo with her knapsack of piss. She made out the trail that followed the old railbed between the trees. It led to a handful of houses, as she knew. There would be someone who might drive her home. She crossed the road. The house on her left was dark, but other houses weren't far away. Taking off her useless hurting shoes, she walked in her stocking feet on snow packed down by snowmobiles. Cold throbbed up into her ankles. Her feet ached. But when she lifted her foot, the cold was gone. The cold burned her foot, she lifted it: there was relief.

On her left was the frozen creek. Snow-laden evergreens on its far side, not the liquid maples being milked by Nan. And she saw her old friend's eyes urging her to come home with her and Jim, but not warning her, not saying avoid this man.

Snowflakes tickled her face, like loose hairs you can't quite see. She brushed them away. A light gleamed through the trees.

"Hail, holy light," Lulu thought. Winnie again. Act two, line one.

She went forward and lost the light. Backtracked, and came up to a road. The road led to a wider opening in the woods, and then the house with the porch light.

At the front door, hesitating, she peered in through the upper pane of glass and saw two people she knew on the sofa, deep in conversation, so intent on each other she guessed they were either at the end of an affair or at the beginning.

She tried the door handle and in she went, like a bad dream.

They sat spellbound, staring at her. Hugh Shapiro and Guy's wife. "What are *you* doing here?" Julie cried, caught out and dismayed.

"Trying to get home, believe it or not."

Hugh took her by the arm and brought her to the woodstove. He took her shoes out of her hand. Helped her off with her coat. Pulled over a chair and helped her to sit down.

Then he sat beside her and held her hand, and Lulu did not let go. But where had he put her coat? Her eyes swung around and caught sight of it on a hook by the door: frosty-white on the back with ice crystals, like Blake's dark wedding jacket.

"Do I smell?" she said.

"No."

How warm it was, how pleasant in this room with its paintings and bookshelves and braided rug on the floor. A piano in the corner. "Those are your paintings," she said.

"Lulu," he said, "what's going on? What happened?"

"I accepted a ride from a psychopath," she said.

She liked the paintings. They weren't mediocre.

"What psychopath?"

"Do I even know what the word means? What does the word mean?"

"Lulu, who are we talking about?"

She turned her head and looked into his worried blue eyes. "Nan's first husband. John Sharpe."

"What did he do to you?"

"Nothing I couldn't handle in the end, I have to say. A scuffle. An altercation. I'll spare you the details."

Julie had been filling a dishpan with warm water. She brought it over and guided Lulu's feet into the warmth. This had happened before, having her feet kindly attended to. Nan had bathed her bloodied foot after she got tangled up in a wire fence at Guy's. Summertime then, and now it was the end of winter.

"I was walking and I saw this opening in the woods, and my Miltonic mind thought, 'Hail, holy light.'" She laughed a little.

"I'll drive you to Nan's after you warm up. Or should I be taking you to the police station in Perth? I can do that," Hugh said.

"Nan's." She was watching her feet inside their sheer pantyhose go from dead-white to bluish-pink in the red dishpan.

Julie brought her a mug of tea. Without letting go of Hugh's hand, Lulu took the mug and said thank you. Then thought to say, "I'd rather this not get around. Don't tell Guy. Or Ducky. Please."

In the long mirror on Nan's bathroom door, Lulu caught a glimpse of herself—her head and shoulders rising above the bathtub, looking steamy and stunned. Hugh had dropped Julie off at the farm first, where Guy would be asleep or pretending to be, she thought. I don't want to know myself either. I don't want to know how I fell into that nightmare or what I should have done instead.

She drifted off until the sound of voices brought her back. They were talking by the fire outside, Hugh Shapiro and Nan and Jim. She got out of the tub and dried herself, went into her room for warm clothes, then downstairs. Slipping on her boots, taking a jacket off a peg, she headed outside.

They fell silent at the sight of her. Young Jim got up. "Lulu, sit here."

"You're a gallant lad," she said, lowering herself into the outdoor chair. "I've always said so."

"Lu," Nan started, and Lulu cut her off.

"I'm all right. Alive and well on this beautiful night, and here with you."

Nan wasn't having it. "You've got to tell us what happened."

Lulu didn't want to talk about it, yet she was talking about it. "What kind of marriage were you in?" she said. She heard the accusation in her voice. "Why didn't you ever say how bad he was?"

Nan's hand went to her forehead, in the old gesture. But then she put both of her hands firmly in her lap and held them there. "Let me take you to the police," she pleaded.

"No. I'm not hurt."

"What *happened*?"

Lulu shook her head, and Nan said, "I can't believe he hurt you."

"He never hurt *you*?"

"But he was charming with everybody else. I'm so sorry, Lu." Nan fell silent.

At last she said, "He was a good father. I have to give him that. And after I left him, he remarried, a nice woman. I thought things were better." She continued in a low and dogged voice, "I think we should go to the police."

"You're wrong. There's not a thing they could do."

"Why? Why do you say that?"

Lulu shrugged. "I know what happened."

"So we do nothing at all? That can't be right."

Lulu was seeing into those years when they'd been out of touch. What Nan had kept hidden out of shame, sparing herself. While leaving me, Lulu thought, wide open to that creep.

"Lu? Talk to us."

"I can't," Lulu said. "I can't talk about it."

You think you're closer to someone than you really are, she thought. Closer than you are, more in the know.

And it was easier to think these blaming thoughts than to wonder about herself. And yet she did wonder about herself. She was an old fool, a sucker for flattery. Humiliating herself, being humiliated. Then clamming up about it. No different in that way from Nan.

Jim reached for the ladle. He gave the front pan a stir and a sweet maple smell came to her in a rush, ravishing her nose. "Anyway," she said, "now I'm a believer in the evil eye too. Like your grandfather," she said to Hugh.

The front door of the woodstove was wide open and she watched the fire, mesmerized by the flames, the sounds, the warmth. For a while nobody spoke. The situation they were in—the fire burning, their wakeful selves, darkness all around—made her feel like a watchman of old posted to some distant frontier. If Macbeth were to stumble upon them, there was nothing he would not understand.

"Nan, it was bad luck," she said.

"I should have made sure you had a ride home."

"Oh, I thought I'd come back with Guy. But he'd already left." She half expected Hugh to say something, explain himself and Julie, but he didn't. "It's not your fault," she said.

"Almost done, I think." Jim was examining the foaming sap in the light of his headlamp.

"Let's pour it off then," Nan said, "and we'll finish it in the morning."

The snow at their feet was eaten away and sooty. Spring was coming. Spring was coming, Lulu thought, and it could have been worse.

Nan made cocoa for everyone, including loitering, lingering Hugh Shapiro. She placed the mugs on a tray next to slices of wedding cake, having rescued the untouched extra sheet of cake and brought it home. "Don't burn your tongues," she cautioned.

Hugh took a sip. "Right. No hurry." He set his mug on the kitchen table. "Cocoa's got a warmth that hangs in the throat."

Lulu held her mug in both hands. "What a peaceful room," she breathed. "I could cry it's so peaceful."

11

IT WAS TUESDAY morning now. Wednesday's performance loomed, and all Lulu could think about was the play. She didn't have room in her head for anything else.

Beckett's lines were the toughest she had ever worked on. There were one hundred and fifty pauses in Winnie's two-act monologue—one hundred and fifty banana peels to slip on, not counting the slippery words themselves, not counting the props, each of which had to make its appearance in time with a specific word or syllable. And none of the usual physical cues were any help because she was buried up to her waist, then up to her neck in a pile of sand. Other actresses had crumbled in the part too, or so she had read. Brenda Bruce claimed she never recovered, and Lulu could believe it. Billie Whitelaw needed three months to get the lines under her belt, only to have them unravel when Beckett kept rewriting the script during rehearsals. Under his pen an "oh well" became an "ah well," a three-dot ellipsis became a four-dot ellipsis, and if Billie said "oh well" instead of the new "ah well," he would bury his head in his hands and groan in anguish.

"Beckett conducted his actors like a metronome," she told Ducky, who had walked over from Guy's to help her run lines. "They had to follow the beat in his head. So you might think 'another heavenly day' would have a sprightly intonation, but no, it had to be delivered in a near-monotone." And she imitated Beckett's battened-down though not unmusical voice, which she had heard in a documentary while doing research about the play.

On the kitchen table she had her rehearsal bag—a stand-in for the black-handled tote bag she used on stage—fitted out with pockets and makeshift props. The all-important rehearsal gun was an old revolver she had borrowed from Guy, since Props would only allow a toy handgun. "But I needed the right weight and the right dimensions." Lulu hefted the revolver in her open palm. "The firing panel's gone, but you'd never know."

"So the stage gun's like that?" said Ducky.

"It's disabled too. They keep it in a locked cupboard backstage."

"Safety," Ducky said.

Lulu nodded. There were rules about guns in the theatre. And still thinking aloud, "Winnie's a romantic married to an infant with a dirty mind. He rarely speaks. Willie."

Ducky giggled. "Willie."

"I know. Beckett's broad as well as subtle. But there are times when Winnie hears *herself*, and self-awareness and sorrow pour in. Then you get poetry."

From the living room came the sound of Jim on the piano, a melody so full of yearning they paused to listen. Lulu didn't recognize the tune, but she felt its effect on her sore and abraded heart and saw its effect on Ducky's face—the giving over to enchantment, like a winter quilt being turned to its summer side. They went into the living room and stood listening.

"That was beautiful," Ducky said, when he took his hands off the keys.

"'Always and Forever.' Pat Metheny."

"I never heard it before."

Jim turned to Lulu and asked with concern, "How are you, Lu?" And Lulu gave him a warning look and said she was fine. "Ducky and I were talking about self-awareness," she went on, "which you think is sexy. Maybe you'll tell us why."

Jim sat still, teasing out his earlier thought. "Self-awareness is nobody's strong suit. But to know who you are and not be pretending to be somebody else—not trying too hard. Knowing who you are and being fine with that."

Lulu sighed. "All I'm ever doing is pretending to be somebody else."

"But you do it by standing to one side of yourself. You know who you are." A smart boy, she thought, and he thinks fast. "People who keep their head," he added.

"Hold their nerve," she agreed.

Jim nodded. "What's most attractive is somebody who knows she's attractive."

"That's not me," Ducky said, and the abject look on her face made Lulu smile, and Jim too.

Lulu lifted the wing of hair away from Ducky's right eye. "My darling, I want to see your whole face. Would you consider a barrette?" Ducky giggled again and Lulu said, "Even sexier is someone smart and funny, who doesn't know how attractive she is for some dark and mysterious reason."

"Courage is sexy," Jim said, doing his part. "Actors are brave. Nothing is more attractive."

Hearing the wistful conviction in his voice, Lulu understood that Jim believed he lacked courage, and it was gnawing away at him. But then nobody thinks they're brave, because most of the time we're not. And the previous night washed over her like the salt sea. She felt dirty and defiled and weak, and steadied herself by putting her hand on the solid piano.

She still hadn't called the theatre. For all they knew, she might have dropped off the face of the earth.

"Jim? What do *you* do when you keep muffing a line?"

He looked down at the keyboard. "I look at the notes and try to understand it. Why am I messing it up? Is my fingering wrong? Am I uncertain about what's coming next? If my mind is elsewhere, what am I thinking about?" He paused. "Am I worrying that I started too late to ever be really good?"

Ducky said, "I think you're great."

He gave her a fond, unconvinced smile. "Or am I thinking about the fingering and not the music? Am I leading with my fingers and not my ear? You try to understand how that bit you're messing up fits into the whole piece. Then you know where you're going and why you're going there."

At the kitchen table dear Ducky stood behind her and kneaded her aching shoulders. Lulu closed her eyes and was back in the rehearsal hall, working with the canvas replica of the set and her special chair, an office chair with extra padding to support her and keep her stationary. For the first act they rolled her into place at the back of the mound and locked the wheels. Then for the second act, they lowered the chair to give the impression she had sunk right down into the earth, and that's when claustrophobia really set in. Part of her problem, at least in the beginning, was not liking Winnie much, this cross between a 1950s housewife and a canary bird who never shut up. But the more she worked on the script, the more she heard Winnie's inner scream.

She had given herself deadlines and marked them on a calendar. Get to page ten by such and such a day, page fifteen a week later. She sounded out every vowel and consonant, built the muscle memory in her lips and tongue, developed a relationship with the words. The horror was all the repetitions—the way the play looped on itself—making it easy to skip whole sections, then not know how to work your way back. So she tried to break it down and figure out what was beneath it all. What did Winnie say every day? What was new that she had never said before? And what was new was the oldest thing of all: feeling forsaken. Calling for help and getting no response.

"You have great hands," she murmured. "If acting doesn't work out, you can be a masseuse."

Ducky's hands went still and Lulu thought, Now why did I say that? She swung around and looked into her niece's stricken face. "Acting will work out. If you're given half a chance, you'll be terrific." And she remembered the child of four whose voice was like a little old man's. "I'm a duck," she had announced to Lulu. And Lulu had replied that she too was a duck. And they had quacked their way down to the lake and along the shore, establishing their unbreakable bond. Now, at seventeen, her niece could pass for twenty or older. She was an old soul.

But what a tough life it was. Her own checkered career was nothing but ups and downs. Lulu thought back to herself as a child happy with a mirror, a windowpane, the blank television screen in which she could see herself acting, dancing, twirling, absorbed in who she would be one day. Roping in her brothers as an audience. Reciting poems from a rock in the river. Then in high school her Joan of Arc earned those unforgettable standing ovations and her ambition was sealed. She would make her life in the theatre, she would be famous. Instead, there had been occasional juicy roles followed by smaller ones and for periods of time none at all, when cobwebs covered her telephone and she drank too much. A working actor, not a star; proud of paying her own way, of turning her hand to whatever came along; but what a lot of persuasion was involved, what a lot of ego repair. Coaxing life and resilience back into herself. Picking herself up off the floor.

And here was Ducky starting out.

Well, maybe it would be different for Ducky. Maybe she would have the necessary luck, drive, fairy dust. Certainly she had the talent. Lulu remembered her tears of pride watching her niece perform. Remembered Guy leaning forward in his seat, light spilling off his face as he drank in his daughter. And this was theatre too, she thought. Being the audience. Watching someone you loved surpass herself on stage.

And so Lulu said again, "You're going to be great." Because that mattered too, having someone believe in you.

After that, the two of them ran her lines and they were all there. She had them. So it's not my memory, she thought. It's fear. Stage fright. I can't rely on myself anymore, which is the beginning of the end.

Ducky said, "You're amazing. Your accent's so good and you never lose it. I'm terrible at accents."

"My ham Irish accent." But Lulu felt gratified and reassured. "You'll learn. And they're not essential. Other things are more important."

"Like what?"

"Vulnerability. Presence. Energy. All of which you have," Lulu said. "You have them in spades."

Then she couldn't help adding, "And find yourself a playwright who writes terrific parts for you. You'll be set for life."

She was thinking of Rita Lafontaine in Michel Tremblay's new play that she had seen in Montreal before rehearsing *Happy Days*. That was probably a mistake—certainly it had done nothing for her confidence hearing the waves of laughter roll towards the stage, watching the audience respond to Rita. What a boon to have a famous playwright writing for you, to have a public that knows you and loves you and has known and loved you for the whole of your acting career. In her seat towards the back, Lulu had felt jealousy come down on her like heavy rain, and she had squinted to check out Rita's bare feet, hoping they were beset by bunions, but even her feet were good. *Le Paradis à la fin de vos jours. The Heaven at the End of Your Days.*

Then in Ottawa, partly inspired by Rita, partly by an audio recording of Madeleine Renaud as Winnie in the French version of *Happy Days*, she had tried to persuade Richard to let her use a French accent. The French Winnie made more sense, she wasn't some Irish caricature, she was a woman of a certain age, rather formal and certainly unhinged, who had been through a world war and was sinking under a final catastrophe. She was delicate and precarious, as France was after the war, and Beckett too, having lived through the war in France.

One of her losing battles. Peggy Ashcroft used an Irish accent; end of discussion. Not even Sal liked her French accent.

In the afternoon Blake came up the steps, a hollow-eyed bridegroom in need of coffee and company. Bethany was asleep, he said. She would probably sleep the afternoon away.

He sat with them at the kitchen table, where Lulu was now helping Ducky with her audition pieces for theatre school, two scenes from *Uncle Vanya*. Crows were making a racket in the trees down by the water. They must have found something, Lulu thought. She wondered what it was.

Ducky was saying how much she loved and identified with Sonya. "She just wants to be near Astrov, but he can't see her because she's so plain."

Lulu had to say, "This is going to be a problem. I hate to say it, darling Ducky, but you're not plain."

"I feel plain. I *am* Sonya," Ducky insisted.

From his side of the table, Blake remarked, "It's a good point. You can be beautiful and feel plain. You can be beautiful and not know it."

"Thank you," Ducky said. Then she blushed and looked down.

"So how would you dress to look plain?" Lulu said, and Ducky raised her eyes and looked around.

"Like Nan."

"I heard that," cried Nan. She had just come inside followed by Jim, and Lulu called over to them, "What are the crows on about?"

"A fox," Jim said. "That's the second time we've seen it."

"They're giving it a hard time," Lulu said to herself. Then turning back to Ducky, "Fair enough. You're an actor. You can dress and fix your hair to look plain, you can hold yourself so it's obvious you feel plain. What's more important—what you can't forget—is that none of these people has slept. So all their emotions are extreme and on the surface."

"That sounds like us," Blake said, bemused.

"Doesn't it." Lulu rested her eyes on his face. And somewhat to her surprise they shared one of those looks of understanding that deepen your sense of someone and shift things onto a different plane. Her own colossal fatigue was mirrored in his eyes.

"I wanted to be an actor for a while," Blake admitted.

His mother was at the sink washing her hands. "You were in those plays at school."

"And Dad had me in a theatre camp one summer."

"I remember," Nan said.

There was the sound of the tap being turned off. Then the crows again.

"Is he still here?" Lulu said evenly.

"Dad? Until Thursday."

The day after tomorrow. "And he's still at your place?"

Blake said he was.

Turning to the window, Lulu thoughtfully rubbed the side of her head, still tender from the vicious yank he had given her hair. She said, "Those crows are driving that poor fox out of its mind."

12

IN THE EVENING she asked to borrow a coat from Nan, saying she wanted to go for a drive to clear her head. "Mine isn't warm enough and neither is the jacket I borrowed last night." Her own pissed-on coat she had shoved into a garbage bag and hidden in the trunk of her car.

Nan went off to the wardrobe in the living room and came back with her mother's fur coat of sheared beaver. "It's never fit me and it's warm. Wear it. Keep it."

Lulu slipped it on. "How do I look?"

Nan stood back and smiled. "Like a movie star of old."

The movie star of old squeezed behind the wheel of her rusty 1999 Toyota Corolla. Back-country roads relaxed her, especially at night, especially when she was alone. The only oncoming car dimmed its lights as it came over a hill, and she actually felt moved by the nighttime courtesy, as if the driver had only kindly intentions towards her. In half an hour she was on the outskirts of Lanark, following the familiar curve into town.

Not a soul was about as she drove down the main street. But here was someone. In the winter you couldn't tell if the bundled-up figure was a man or a woman. But the bulkiness and gait were unmistakable. She pulled over.

"I'm escaping the uproar," he said, sliding in beside her, in cahoots with her once again. "I borrowed Roseanne's car and drove into town, and I've been walking around."

Lulu put her car in park and left the motor running. "What uproar?"

"Blake's bombshell," Tony said.

He didn't go on and she wondered if she was going to have to dig with her bare hands for every scrap of information. "Start at the beginning," she said.

No problem. He and Roseanne were staying with Janet at the farm, and Blake had dropped by and announced two things: first, that Bethany was pregnant, and second, that he was leaving the church. "Janet had an egg flipper in her hand. I thought she was going to beat him with it."

So the cat was deep among the pigeons. "Did he say what he's going to do?"

"He's giving up the church, but keeping his job. Whatever that is."

"Teaching at the elementary school," she said.

"I was walking around, remembering," he said. "Nothing much has changed."

"*You* have."

His guffaw was the kind of response you hope for on opening night. "So have you," he said to her.

"How?" Unable to resist. Men can resist that question, she thought, but women never can. "Don't answer that."

"You're more beautiful than ever," Tony said.

They were parked beside a considerable snowbank and Lulu felt herself come apart. "Don't be stupid," she whispered. She closed her eyes on tears.

"You've done well without me," he said.

"Yes. I have."

They had the street entirely to themselves—the town, entirely to themselves.

"Lu, where were we living when the old guy on the third floor drowned in his bathtub?"

"Baldwin Street."

"Baldwin. I couldn't remember."

Their hippie house in Toronto. 1970. That was when she was in the hospital with hepatitis and Nan came to visit with a bag of oranges. She didn't see her again until they reconnected at the lake during the long, hot summer of 1995, when Canada too was on the verge of coming apart.

She said, "We were pretty wild in those days. Some of the things we did." She was thinking of the drugs and chaos and communal living, and of Nan's comparative primness. Word of her marriage had come to Lulu third-hand and she had assumed it was Nan falling in line, embracing her conservative self, when in fact it was Nan in flight, finding a way to have her child.

"I feel sorry for Blake," she said. "I'm sorry for them both."

"Well, they made their bed," Tony said.

His dismissive words cut into her and she turned away. "We're not very happy, are we?"

"I've never found it," he said.

"Happiness?"

"Love."

"Right. You wanted love in your life I remember."

"My children love me." He rummaged in his coat pocket. "They love me unconditionally."

"Lucky you," she said.

He pulled out his cellphone and she guessed what was coming. Sure enough he was showing her his sons, two good-looking men in their twenties, dark-haired, tanned, their arms flung around each other.

"Joe and Ned," he told her.

"They look like you." She scrolled ahead to find them side by side in a café, all grins and easy affection, and Tony's winning ways in bed flooded back, how relaxed he was and never in a hurry; also his thieving ways, the pride he took in slipping things into his pocket, cigarettes, packets of gum, spools of thread for his mother: keeping his hand in, he called it. "How's your mother?" she asked. "How's Eleanor?"

"Not great. Full of arthritis. A friend lives with her and helps her get around. They share a house in Vancouver."

"So that's what you tell customs when you fly in from Bangkok? You're visiting your elderly mother who needs you. And who's this?" Turning the screen to show him the sleek young man with pieces of gold spread out like a deck of cards.

"I like to have proof I've handed over the gold." He took back his phone and slid it into his pocket.

"It's not risky to have that on your phone? You're not afraid of getting caught?"

"Here? Canadian laws are so lax money launderers never get caught."

"Is that true?"

He assured her it was. Canada was one of the easiest places in the world to launder money. "It's a well-known fact. You're shivering," he said. "Here, warm yourself on me." He slipped off her gloves and put his hands around hers. Old times, she thought. She never would have recognized his face, but she recognized his touch.

"Did my sleeping pills help?" he wanted to know.

She had forgotten all about them. They must have been lost in the struggle somewhere, either in the car or on the snowy ground. "I haven't tried them," she said. His hands were warm. Lovely. Stroking and rubbing hers.

"I've missed you, Lu."

She couldn't help but smile. What a pair they were.

"Is it too late for us?" he said.

It was less question than invitation. And what was wrong with taking comfort where you found it? Who were they to be fussy?

She said, "What about your Sherry? To say nothing of good old Roseanne."

"Come with me," he said.

"Where?"

"Bangkok."

"Bangkok," she repeated.

"I own six apartments," he said. "I own the building."

"Oh, Tony," she said. "You're such a dink. I'll be a kept woman in one of your apartments?"

"You could come and go. I'm back and forth all the time."

"And this would be love," she said.

He still had her hands in his warm and comforting grip. Now, as if offering a bouquet of roses, he confided that he had a collection of Tibetan book covers worth half a million dollars. "They're works of art," he said proudly. "Hundreds of years old."

"More money laundering?" She took back her hands.

And he conceded they were a great investment.

"Where have you stashed them?"

"I rent a storage shed on Janet's farm."

"That's my boy," she said. Tibetan book covers in the Ontario backwoods. He had gone from collecting old books and not reading them to collecting ancient book covers he didn't have to read. "And you tell her they're religious art, so she gives you a big fat discount."

She leaned in and kissed his furry cheek. "Stay out of jail," she said.

13

AWAKE AT DAWN, she went to her bedroom window and stood watching as darkness gave up the ghost. Briefly, the snow was a blue petal lit from within. Then more like a pearl.

She was remembering her dream. She had forgotten the name of the play she was in and nobody would tell her what it was. She approached one person after another and without exception they turned their backs on her.

Which actress was it?—to whom Beckett admitted that the germ of the play came from wondering what would be the most dreadful thing that could happen to a person, and it would be sinking into the ground alive, the sun glaring down, no shade at all, no possibility of sleep because a bell rings you awake whenever you drop off, "And all you've got is a little parcel of things to see you through life. And I thought who would cope with that and go down singing, only a woman."

She had heard his voice just the once, in that documentary about his life. A soft, hesitant, crumbling voice, malleable and warm, without a hint of harshness or dryness. But he didn't fold that voice into his plays. Instead, he chose to drive his characters up against a razor fence. She had read extracts of his letters in the biography she'd been lugging around for the last two months—and he was a great comforter, nobody kinder, nobody more eloquent in his kindness. But he wouldn't allow himself the liberties of kindness and comfort in his plays, because he was dead set on less and less. Subtracting, losing, impoverishing, *not* knowing. Embracing what he called the poetic void. But *more* makes for less too, she thought. More panic. More snow. The deeper they are, the less there is of anything else.

The snow had the glimmer of eggshells now—that kind of light. The field sloped down on the left to apple trees and a split-rail fence.

As a young man, he ran over the family dog. They were alike in that lamentable way. She too had backed up over a beloved pet and never forgiven herself. Poor Pog, buried over there near the apple trees.

She went downstairs in her dressing gown, her cellphone in her pocket, and found Ducky in her nightgown at the kitchen table. Sometimes Ducky slept at her father's, sometimes here. Lulu brought out her phone and stared at it. "Is it still as hard as ever to get reception here?"

Ducky nodded. But she had seen people getting a signal just below the little white church. "Where the wooden garage is. They pull in there."

Lulu closed her eyes for a moment. She never did call Sal to tell her where she was, and now it was Wednesday. I'm a coward, she thought, a craven coward.

"You didn't sleep?" Ducky said.

She put her phone on the table. "I'm afraid of bad news. I'm afraid to turn it on. Anyway, it's too early to call. I'll wait a bit."

She sat down and reached across and lifted Ducky's hair out of her eyes. "Why did you say you *are* Sonya?"

Ducky blushed. "Oh."

Her niece's flannel nightgown was inside out.

"I've always considered myself a loner," Ducky said with an effort. "And sometimes that's all right. I'm wary around people."

"You're not wary around us."

"With friends at school," Ducky said. "It's hard for me to make friends. I have friends, but I'm never sure they really want to be friends with me. I mistrust every word they say." Tears oozed around her eyes. "Sonya feels alone too."

Lulu waited until the tears eased off. "You'll make a great Sonya. But you're not alone. You're loved. And so was Sonya. She was lovable and loved and loving. Like you."

"I'm not so sure I'm loving." Disbelieving, mortified.

They heard movement upstairs. Nan.

"Darling? I've been meaning to ask if you'd rather be called Irene."

"I love it when you call me Ducky."

"And when I call you darling? Does it sound affected?"

"Not when you say it."

Lulu gave her niece's hand a squeeze. The night before, after driving back from Lanark, she and Nan had fallen into a midnight conversation that turned partly on her overuse of "darling," with Nan saying she could no more say "darling" than fly to the moon; only rich people said "darling" when she was growing up. And Lulu defended it as a playful word, a theatre word, a useful word. Sometimes it meant hello. Sometimes it meant I love you. Sometimes, I hate you. Sometimes, I don't trust you.

"Darling?" she had then said provocatively. "Remember when I was sick with hepatitis and you brought me oranges? Why didn't you come back? I didn't see you again for a quarter of a century."

They were at the kitchen table and Nan's body sank a little in her chair. "You had all your hippie friends," she said at last. "It was never my thing, drugs and sex and granny glasses. I didn't fit in at all." She twisted her wedding band around her finger. "I was straight and you thought I was boring."

Lulu nodded. She didn't deny it.

"We went down different paths," Nan said. "It happens. And then you showed up again out of the blue, and like I always tell you, our friendship is one of the best things in my life." She was still working her wedding band around her finger.

"Darling, throw that thing into the snow."

Nan looked down at her hands. She covered her left hand with her right and put them in her lap. "Have you been holding that against me all these years?"

"Not all these years." Lulu looked away, then said abruptly, "Tony Lloyd tells me your old enemy is going nuts. Blake announced he's leaving the church. He's through with it."

Nan went still. "Why? What happened?"

"All I know is that he told his in-laws he's leaving the church and that Bethany is pregnant. Janet nearly killed him."

"Good for him," Nan said. "He's been unhappy for the longest time. I wonder when he decided. I know so little about him."

"He's very private," Lulu said. "Even more so than Jim."

"Of course." Nan's voice sharpened with pain. "But that explanation doesn't explain. The question I want an answer to is *why* they're so private."

"Well now, where do you suppose they get it from?"

Nan stared at her.

"Nobody can keep a secret like you can," Lulu said.

Nan took off her glasses and rubbed her eyes. "I guess that's true. I hadn't thought of that." She said, "Who knew Blake had girlfriends? I thought he lived like a monk."

"You know, I'm starting to like him. There's more to him than I realized."

Nan's face softened. "Do you think so?" Her grateful eyes rested on Lulu. "You look so tired, Lu. I'm keeping you up. You should be in bed."

"Tony gave me sleeping pills and I went and lost them." Her laugh was almost merry. "My gold-smuggling drug-pusher of an ex-boyfriend."

"You sound like a girl when you laugh, Lu. I love your laugh." Then Nan said, "You're as bad as Jim. You won't tell me things. You leave me to my worst imaginings." She persisted, "I wish you'd tell me what happened."

"And I wish you wouldn't ask."

Nan was silent. Then, "I'm sorry." She got to her feet and stood looking down at Lulu. "You'll be fine tomorrow night. Don't worry."

"Either I'll be fine or I'll be terrible."

"You won't be terrible. You're always good."

"Am I, darling? I wish I believed you."

She had always felt more in the know than Nan. Older by two years. At school they were in the same class, Lulu having been held back a year because know-it-all Ontario didn't trust the schools in the Yukon. In Lanark they had rescued each other and been inseparable, riding the bus back and forth to high school in Perth, and when Nan moved away three years later—when Lulu first heard the news—she had been physically sick.

They had met up again at university—same city, but different schools miles apart, so their contact was infrequent and they had both changed. Their reunion in late middle age still seemed like one of life's miracles. It had occurred to Lulu that part of their enduring bond was her deep fondness for Jim, just as her love for Ducky had healed the rift with Guy. Love the child and the friendship flows.

Lulu saw in Nan a great carefulness, living alone in the woods, taking pains not to have an accident. And emotionally careful—not to hurt and not to put herself in a position of being hurt. No plunging into perilous waters. Careful.

Of course there was such a thing as overcaution, the ruination of many a performance; Richard in rehearsals telling her *not* to think. Nan overthought and didn't tell you what you needed to know. Such as, I was in an abusive marriage. Such as, Don't get in a car with this man.

Now, in the morning light of Wednesday, great fat snowflakes were sailing past the kitchen windows like relaxed, big-hipped women. How restful it was to look out and see the sumptuous life they were having.

And finally she reached for her cellphone and turned it on.

Ducky was right. No reception. She didn't want to be overheard on the kitchen phone. And besides, she needed to get her messages. She would have to drive to the garage below the church.

14

THE WOODEN GARAGE was more like a small barn. In front
of it there was space for just one car and she pulled in. On her
left, fields sloped down towards a wide stretch of woods beyond
which was the Mississippi River. On her right, in the near distance, there used to be a magnificent elm next to the train
station, its vast umbrella shape a landmark for miles around.
Her mother had treasured the tree. But in the late 1970s it suc-
cumbed to Dutch elm disease and eventually half a dozen men
with chainsaws took it down. Behind her, on the other side of
the road, were the sand and gravel pits that had been carving
up the edge of the village for as long as she could remember.
A toboggan hill had been swallowed up and spat out, as well as
various fields and ridges and stands of white pine, all the sand
and gravel used mainly for roads, as if one-third of the fate of
Snow Road Station had been written in its name.

She reached into her pocket for her cellphone. Moments later she got reception and checked her messages. Then she sat on behind the wheel for a while. Life comes in waves, she thought. You're not wanted, then you're wanted, then you're not wanted anymore.

Back at Nan's she kicked off her boots and hung up her glamorous fur coat before turning to face them. She held out her phone. "They couldn't reach me," she said. "They gave up on me. I've been axed."

Jim had been about to take a sip of coffee. He set down his mug.

Nan lowered herself into the chair beside him. "Can they do that?"

Ducky, still in her nightgown, stared at her.

Five messages from the same number, building in urgency. Sal was calling her in for an emergency rehearsal. Then asking where she was. Then, where the hell was she. Then, if you don't respond, we'll get someone else. Then, we've got someone else.

"How can I blame them?" she cried. "I never told them I was here." Massaging her chest with both hands, she lost her grip on the black evil tidings, which tumbled to the floor.

Her misery had Jim pleading, "Don't be sad. Be mad. That's what you always say."

Nan came over to her and put her arms around her, and Lulu pressed her face into Nan's shoulder. Then she took a step back. "But I'm sad, Jim. I'm unbelievably sad." She bent down and scooped up the cellphone. "This thing," she said.

She went over to the table and slammed it down next to a bowl of oranges.

In Nan's fur coat, she headed on foot down the lane and out to the road. "I'll be back," she said, reassuring their hangdog faces and reminding herself of her mother when the Klondike River went into flood. "I'll be back," her mother had promised, after which Lulu lined up her brothers and herself on the sofa in their orange life jackets, and waited. Only five years old. A long, long time ago. Eventually, her mother reappeared, having moved their car to safety. The sight of them sitting in a row regarding her with big serious eyes got immortalized in a framed snapshot that sat on their piano from then on.

At the end of the lane, she turned left with nothing in mind beyond trudging along beside the head-high drifts. At the top of a rise she paused. Below lay a sheltered field, unfenced, and she took herself there. What she wanted was to fall backwards into its mattressy depths—spread her length across the field and lie quiet for a while. But a bank of snow barred her way, so she scrambled up its side and sank in up to her knees. Jesus H. Christ. Back on the road she emptied out her boots. Then, intent on the same comfort, she let herself fall backwards into the snowbank and instantly the snow moulded itself to her back and bottom like a bronze cast. She sat erect on a hard throne.

Somehow in all these years of living she had forgotten that soft snow packs into a hard thing. It was nearly the end of March. The sun beat down with such warmth that she closed her eyes and let it bathe her face.

When she opened her eyes, a fox was observing her from across the road.

She said softly, "*Bonjour*-Hi, *Monsieur* Fox."

Sharp-pointed ears, and white around the muzzle and under the throat; otherwise rusty-orange against the snow.

"What should I do with the rest of my life?" she said. "What would you advise?"

The fox looked over its shoulder, then back at her, its ears ever alert. From above came a light dusting of snow from a tall white pine. Snow motes like gold dust, falling here and nowhere else. Sing your song, Winnie. Sing your song. And sitting on her hard throne, Lulu sang to the fox. "*Every touch of fingers / Tells me what I know, / Says for you, / It's true, it's true, / You love me so!*"

The big, plushy tail sailed out of sight—a bounding and a disappearance.

More flecks of snow drifted down, brighter than the bright air. Who had they found to replace her? Who knew the part well enough to step in at almost no notice? Well, Richard hadn't wanted her anyway; if the first Winnie hadn't backed out when Stratford came calling, he would never have hired her.

Getting out of the throne wasn't easy. She had to push with her feet and hands, which filled her boots and mitts with snow. But she got herself upright, then took off her coat and shook out the sleeves. Shook out her boots. Stood looking down at her soup tureen of a bottom, and from deep inside her there came a groan of shame so overwhelming she closed her eyes and bowed her head. Not calling Sal: that was unconscionable.

Awful. Shoving her hands into the unfamiliar pockets, she trudged on, her eyes fixed on the narrow road made narrower by snowbanks and snow-laden trees, as pretty as an old-fashioned Christmas card or a picture-book road that casts a spell over a child. She trod the twists and turns she knew by heart until a vigorous tapping brought her out of herself. About eight feet away, a pileated woodpecker the size of a crow was gouging chunks out of a tree. It turned its head and gave her a bloody grin—the long red stripe on its cheek as livid as its red crest—before it resumed its disembowelling business of making a huge hole even huger.

At Guy's laneway, she turned in. His back door opened into a mud room beyond which was the ample kitchen. She had expected a bark or two of greeting from Sheba, his St. Bernard, but silence. In the kitchen she stood in her stocking feet, surveying the lake from the big bay window. Tracks led across the snowy ice. Human and dog. Then she heard a laugh or a sob. She heard it again. It came from the living room.

Guy was at his wide desk in the corner, his back to her. Sheba lay stretched out at his feet.

"Are you all right?" she asked. She had caught him shoving his handkerchief into his back pocket, but his face was cheerful when he turned around.

"I am. I didn't hear your car."

"I walked." She went over to him. "Were you crying? I thought I heard you weeping."

"I might have been." He smiled. He looked greyer and heavier. His desk was strewn with books and papers.

"Why the tears?" she said.

"I don't know. First I read one book, then another. It's a weepy day." And he smiled at her again. "But thank you for coming to ask," he said.

Lulu sank into the nearest chair, thinking how odd and private we are and insist on being. How little we know about each other, even when we know a lot. It hurt her that he was keeping himself to himself, yet how little she ever told him either.

She said, "I finally checked my messages. I should have checked them earlier. I've been canned."

"From your play? Then they're idiots," he said.

She couldn't agree with him, but how much better she felt for hearing him say so. "It's my fault," she said. "I've been forgetting my lines."

"So what? That's what prompters are for. Fight back, Lu."

She looked away, wondering if she had it in her. "Where is everybody? Where's Julie?"

"She's gone."

She stared at him, seeing the tracks across the bay. "Where?"

"To her mother's in Kingston." Guy flipped over a piece of paper on his desk, then turned it face down again. "Or so she says."

Lulu touched his knee, and he took her hand and held it.

"I can drive you back to Nan's," he said. "Then you can head on to Ottawa. And don't let them push you around."

They heard Janet's clarion voice as they went up the steps at Nan's. The house was crowded, Lulu would think later, and the crowd was Janet. She had her arms folded across her massive bosom and was demanding explanations about Blake's behaviour. Nan had none to give.

Lulu saw the bewildered look on her brother's face. "Somebody fill me in," he said.

She left them to it. Grabbing her cellphone from beside the oranges, she headed upstairs where for a moment she sat on the edge of her bed, wired but exhausted. Then she gathered up her handbag and her rehearsal bag, and the suitcase she had packed that morning, and carried them down to the kitchen. She gave farewell hugs to her brother and Jim, then to Nan and Ducky. A nod in Janet's direction, and she was on her way.

At the main road, instead of turning in the direction of Ottawa, she went back to the garage below the church and got reception, as she had earlier. She called Sal, who failed to pick up, so she left a message, saying she would be at the theatre by six o'clock. "As usual, Sal. Doing my warm-up."

It was March 26th and it was snowing again. For a moment Lulu watched the flakes drift down on the garage and the fields and the woods and the village. A little after one o'clock. There was time for one more detour.

15

BLAKE'S CAR WASN'T in his driveway, but John Sharpe's rental car was, not a vehicle she would easily forget. She pulled in behind it and reached for her bag. Her knees warned her she was making another mistake. So did her pounding heart. But she couldn't just leave it, she had to get some of her own back.

She got out and made her way around Sharpe's SUV to Blake's front door. Without knocking, she entered the house.

Sometimes, when she couldn't remember a line, she would try to fish the words out of the void by making throat sounds—coughs, grunts, humming, nonsense sounds—anything to coax the words into view. She had seen actors turn themselves inside out in the same desperate effort. Other times she went absolutely still, hoping silence would work in her favour. Bethany's voice was coming from the kitchen into the front hallway, where hooks lined either side like a cloakroom for the upper grades. Lulu slipped off her boots, hung her fur coat by its loop on one of the hooks, stepped forward to the kitchen doorway.

They were at the table and didn't notice her. Sharpe had his back to her. Bethany was out of sight on his left. The fridge was loud, the stove had seen better days, the kitchen counter had enough mugs for a small church gathering. The whole place had a boarding-house smell.

Bethany was saying, "I don't know about that, but she's nice."

"That's not my experience."

"It's not?"

"I don't think she's nice."

Lulu entered on her quiet feet and put her hand on the culprit's shoulder. "Are you singing my praises again?"

His head jerked back so abruptly he nearly tipped over his chair, and she burst out laughing. She couldn't remember the last time she had laughed so hard. It did her a world of good.

His eyes narrowed. "If it isn't Lulu Blake," he said, "the bad old girl."

She set her bag on the kitchen table, pulled out a chair and sat down. Noticing the bandage on his hand, she smiled. "Did I draw blood?" Her voice was steady, even if her hands were not.

He leaned towards her, back in charge, easy with himself again. "Too bad you lost your nerve the other night. I figured an old babe like you would enjoy a little fun." He shrugged. "So what do you want now? Kiss and make up?"

"Money," Lulu said. "My coat's ruined. So are my shoes."

"Not my problem."

"I thought you might say that." She opened her bag and took out the revolver and pointed it at his chest.

He stared at the gun. Raised his eyes and stared at her with gratifying alarm.

Bethany let out a hiccup and clapped her hand over her mouth.

Lulu smiled again. All her nervousness was gone.

Slowly, reluctantly, he reached into the pocket of his jeans, dug his long fingers deep and tugged. Finally, the wallet came. "I've only got American," he said.

"That's fine," she said.

He opened the dark leather wallet and riffled through his cash. "You're a crazy woman."

Bethany was all eyes and hiccups. Lulu gave her a wink without letting Sharpe's hands out of her sight.

"Five hundred will do it." Her voice held steady and for that she had a lifetime of monologues to thank.

He spread green bills on the table. Canadians think ten-dollar bills are purple, Americans think all guns are loaded; and that's the difference between Canadians and Americans, she thought.

"Count it," he said.

"You count it."

"There's four hundred. It's all I have on me."

If she reached for it, he would grab her wrist.

"Bethany," she said. "Do me a favour. Put the money into my bag."

Bethany got to her feet, and in the same moment the front door opened and Blake called out that he was back. Bethany stood frozen, her head turned in the direction of Blake's voice. Lulu seized the moment to scoop up the money and drop it into her bag along with the gun. Then Blake was in the doorway, staring at them. "What's up?"

"Your father and I had an account to settle," Lulu said.

She was already moving into the hallway when Sharpe spoke behind her. "I remember now. Nan used to talk about you."

She heard him shove his chair back from the table. Heard him say, "She said you were an actor who would never be great."

Lulu set her bag on the floor next to her boots and bent down to pull them on, aware of his every movement.

"She went to see you in a play." He was in the doorway now. "You were so bad she didn't go backstage afterwards."

Lulu lifted her coat off its hook.

"She was going to surprise you. But she didn't know what to say. So she came home and said to me, 'I thought she'd be better.'"

Lulu had her coat on and was struggling with the buttons when he delivered his final taunt: "So I guess you're a better drama queen than an actor."

Something snapped inside her. She strode up to him and stood in his face. "Shall I tell Blake and Bethany what you did to me?" She rammed her finger into his chest. The heat of her anger could have burned the house down. "Stop. Fucking. With. Me. You Fucking Asshole."

He backed away under the force of her jabbing finger and she saw Blake at his shoulder, wide-eyed and staring, and Bethany cowering behind.

Turning on her heel, she made for the front door, yanked it open and stepped outside. There was a buildup of snow and ice on the threshold; she had to tug hard to pull the door shut behind her. Then the cold air washed over her and carried her waves of adrenalin out to sea.

I thought she'd be better. That had the sad ring of truth.

At least she had his money. She had the look on his face when she pulled the gun on him. She had him backing away from her fury. She had the pleasure of landing her lines like a pro.

16

AN HOUR LATER she was coming into Ottawa, wondering what she could tell them. That she had needed to disappear for a while and not be found? That she couldn't explain it? They would say she had set herself up to be fired, and maybe she had. You can want something and not want it at the same time. You can want a role, a child, a cherry orchard more than anything in the world, yet not want them at all.

Passing road signs in French and English, she thought of René Lévesque's unforgettable face, so rumpled and full of feeling, his mournful eyes, his hair combed over to hide his baldness. Her sentimental favourite for having fought rather nobly for Quebec independence and lost. In the end he had to fall back on what he called *le beau risque* of a renewed federalism. That's what she was going to have to do too. Swallow her pride, and ask Richard and Sal to give her another chance.

The traffic had picked up. It was almost four o'clock, already rush hour, but she was going into the city rather than leaving, so her speed didn't slacken.

A few minutes after five o'clock, her rehearsal bag over her shoulder, she braved the stage door and entered the warren of fluorescent corridors. The double set of black rehearsal-hall doors were immediately on her left. She felt her knees buckle, knowing who had to be in there and how unwelcome she would be. So she followed the corridor to her dressing room, intending to sit down and collect herself.

All her things were gone. Even the wooden chair Sal had filched from an upstairs office because it was better for her back—gone. At her dressing station, in front of the mirror, arranged on a white towel like a prissy little island of composure, were makeup bag, comb, face cream, tissues, hand mirror. None of them hers.

She swung around, retraced her steps, and hauled open the rehearsal-hall door. There they were, Richard and Sal side by side, and across from them Olivia Shorter. Of course. Olivia and Richard—old Toronto pals. They stared at her, open-mouthed. Then Richard exchanged a glance with Sal, and Sal was gripping her arm, steering her back into the corridor. She heard Richard say, "Keep going, Olivia. That was lovely."

"Where were you?" Sal hissed. "You left without signing out. You didn't answer your phone."

"I'm here now. I'm ready to go."

"It's too late." Sal's face was even rosier than her hair.

Lulu felt a sharp pain behind her eyes. "Look," she said. "People forget to sign out all the time. You know they do. Have

I ever failed you? I haven't been late once, not to a rehearsal, not to a performance."

"Well, you're three days late to this one. We called an emergency rehearsal on Sunday. We've been here since Monday. I phoned you five times. Why are we even talking about this?"

The door opened. Whip-thin Richard looked past her and summoned Sal: "We need you in here."

The fluorescent lights bleached his face and drained the hot-pink from Sal's hair. All these weeks of working underground, eating sandwiches in the dreary little green room, returning to the tyranny of her mound of dirt.

Lulu pressed her rehearsal bag to her side. "We're talking."

He gave her a long, stabbing look with his dark, exhausted eyes. "What could you possibly have to say to us now?"

"You can't do this, Richard. You can't dump me in the middle of the run. Look, I know I was out of touch. But I was somewhere with no phone connection." Her mouth was dry. She forged ahead. "I was working on the play. I was relearning these crazy lines."

Richard stared at her. Then he turned towards Sal and held the door wide.

Sal cried out, "What else could we do? You weren't at the hotel. You weren't in Montreal. We almost called the police."

"You could have had faith in me," Lulu said.

Now they both stared. Lulu felt the gun in her bag digging into her side. How she would have loved to pull it out and wipe the sour condescension off Richard's face.

"Am I drunk?" she said. "Stoned? Out of my mind? I've been working on my lines for three days. You said the break would do me good. And it did."

Sal's mouth was open, but it was Richard who spoke. "A decision has been taken," he said.

Silence.

Then Lulu said, "Fuck you, Richard."

"Wait," Sal said. "I've got your stuff in my office."

She set off at a half run and was unlocking the stage manager's door when Lulu caught up with her.

"That wasn't good," Sal muttered.

"He's a bastard."

"He's furious. Where were you, anyway?" Sal pushed the door open. "We've been in touch with Equity. You should be too."

"Now there's a sad sight," said Lulu. On Sal's desk were two plastic bags into which her things had been unceremoniously dumped.

"I can't believe you haven't apologized," Sal said.

Lulu stood still. "You know I'm sorrier than I can possibly say."

"Oh, Lulu." Sal took a deep breath. "Listen," she sighed, "I have to say this. Please don't come back to the theatre."

Lulu stared at her.

"We'll be in touch through Equity," Sal went on in a rush. "They'll mediate the end of your contract and you'll be paid." She came forward as if to offer a quick hug. "I have to get back."

"I'm better than Olivia."

"She's very good, Lulu." Sal was ushering her and her bags out the door.

"I'm a better actor. You know I am."

Sal stopped in her tracks. "You couldn't remember your lines."

Plastic bags in one hand, rehearsal bag in the other, Lulu stood next to the canal that ran past the theatre's broad backside. The dilapidated ice was another sad sight—a study in breakup and rot. This would soon be going the rounds. "She blanked on her lines. She disappeared." "They had to bring in Olivia Shorter. Olivia was amazing."

Closing her eyes, Lulu saw her dressing station overtaken by Olivia's crap, and the visual blow landed a hard second punch, decades old, of switching on the light in Tony's bathroom to see another woman's earrings on the back of the toilet. So it takes a matching pain to wake up the earlier one. Friction, she thought. Two sticks to start a fire.

The earrings were gold loops, she remembered. There was a cloth cosmetic bag beside them and a pale-green case of contraceptive pills on the edge of the sink. No risk of pregnancy here. She hadn't thought about that episode in a long time—her drunken, boisterous, late-night invasion of Tony's place after the run of *One Night Stand*, when she outlasted nearly everyone at the cast party, and then found herself within a block of his second-floor walk-up on Queen Street. Eldon Cohen was with her, dear Eldon who died a dozen years later of AIDS. They stood giggling on the sidewalk, pressing Tony's bell; he came down in bare feet and jeans, surly and irked. But she ignored his pissy mood until she went down the hall to his bathroom half an hour later, and noticed a faint light shining from under the closed bedroom door. She flicked on the bathroom light and the shoe dropped on her head.

"What an image," breathed Eldon, always the set designer, after she hurried him out of there and described the gold loops on the back of the toilet.

Eastertime then too, she remembered. And turning away from the canal, she saw Ferris heading to the stage door, arriving earlier than usual. He must have spotted her, so intent was he on keeping his head down. He would be hating her guts too. She was sorry, because she liked him. He had helped her run lines until they were punch-drunk. "Oh, you missed something there," he would say, and they had rolled about, laughing their heads off. Then when the play got its bad review, he told her it wasn't a bad review, it was a bad review*er*. Now watching him disappear inside, while she remained out in the cold, she remembered homeless Hazel's shopping cart piled high with overfilled plastic bags, like the ones digging into her hands. Beckett would have liked Hazel. He had a soft spot for anyone down and out, poor constipated bugger. What was the old joke? Joyce couldn't see, Wilde couldn't hear, and Beckett couldn't shit.

Squaring her shoulders, Lulu set off towards her hotel, only to change her mind and head across Confederation Park towards Elgin Street and the Mayflower Pub, her local. Certain cities were known for their air of failure, and she liked them for that very reason. Others were known for their rain, their wind, their sprawl, their skyline, their carnal liberties. This city, named for the mighty river, was known for being easy to escape.

"I've escaped," came the thought.

And what rolled over her, like a heavenly tractor ploughing her old self under, was a sense of freedom and peace unlike anything she had ever known. All her life she had persevered, keeping her hand in come what may. She had never known the pure joy of giving up. Now euphoria filled her body like a rave review.

The long struggle was over.

Coming towards her was a woman in a red beret carrying a boxed cake. The woman smiled a broad, enchanting smile, as if they were in on the same celebratory secret, and Lulu smiled back, singled out by the stranger's overflowing warmth.

Sweet are the uses of adversity, Lulu thought, *which, like the toad*, something something something *wears yet a precious jewel in his head*. And it seemed to her that a better life, a better person, lay within reach.

Turning south on Elgin Street, she passed the corner church where a few pots of Easter flowers had toppled over in the wind, and she heard her name being called. Across the street four people were waving at her with wild abandon.

Setting down her bags, she raised her arms and waved joyously in return.

The foursome crossed over and crowded around her in the early evening sun. Nan's arms were full of red tulips. "We bought out the store," she crowed, "every tulip they had."

"Darlings, you've come for the play, but I'm not in it."

"We've come for you," Guy said.

Lulu lowered her face to the blooms that Nan pressed into her arms. A bouquet of friends—of family, in fact. Brother, niece, almost-sister, and Jim. Her eyes welled up and over. She had to bury her wet face in the crook of her arm. "Silly."

Jim smiled. "Silly is good."

He picked up her bags as Guy threw his arm around her and they trooped into the Mayflower, where the waiter brought a pail of water for her armful of tulips and positioned them on the floor next to their booth.

"They're beautiful, Nan. Springtime."

Guy leaned forward. "So what happened? Did you talk to them?"

"Sure," Lulu said, "I talked to them." She paused, taking in their expectant faces.

"What did they say?"

"They said, 'A decision has been taken.'"

"What assholes," said Guy.

"And what did *you* say?" said Nan.

Lulu smiled a wry smile. "To have faith in me."

Nan's face softened and she nodded. "That's good."

"It made no difference."

"No, but it's good."

Jim had a glint in his eye. "So you didn't pull your gun on them?"

Word got around fast. "Oh, I was tempted, just to give them a scare. They know it doesn't shoot, though." But Jim was waiting for a full confession, as were the others. "Okay," she said, "who told you?"

"Blake. He said you pulled a gun on John Sharpe."

"Did he tell you why?"

"Something about throwing up in John's car, all over your coat, and you expected him to pay for the dry cleaning."

"What a liar." Lulu's harsh retort had other customers glancing over. "Do you want the ugly truth?" she said. "He peed on me."

They stared at her in disbelief, and she nodded, "I resisted his advances so he shoved me out of his car and drove off. Then I heard him coming back and hid in the ditch." She saw the shock in their faces and wondered if they doubted her. "But he found me," she said, "and peed all over my back."

"Christ," Guy said. "That is vile."

"Yes," she said. "It was. It is, every time I think about it."

The young server arrived at the table with their tray of drinks. "You folks all right?" he said, setting out their glasses of beer. No one answered until Guy raised his hand and waved him away.

Nan sat like stone. She looked grey and old in the fading light that came through the dusty window beside them.

"I shouldn't have told you," Lulu said.

"No," Nan stared at the glass in front of her, "not knowing is worse. You have to understand what you're dealing with." She raised her eyes. "But how will I ever make it up to you?"

Lulu reached across the table and put her hand on Nan's. "Hey. Look at me. What do you see?"

"My old friend," Nan said, "who's not okay."

Lulu's eyes welled up and she coughed and reached for her glass.

"Oh, Lu," Nan said.

No one spoke.

Then Nan said, "Didn't you rent out your apartment? You don't have anywhere to go right now."

Guy leaned forward. "You can stay with me."

Lulu looked into the eyes of her brother and saw some-one else whose life had gone off the rails. "There's plenty of room," he said. "You'll have the house to yourself for a while." He was taking Ducky back to Toronto in the morning and would stay on in the city for a week or so.

"I thought the only view of Toronto you liked was the one in your rear-view mirror."

He flashed her a grin and rubbed his nose. "Change of scene."

Lulu turned her face to the window. It would be dark soon, the roads empty, the night cold and clear, and all of it would be familiar, as if she were going home.

She said to Guy, "What about your sugar bush? What about your animals?"

"I've got two men looking after them." Her brother gave her a teasing smile. "And one of them you know."

1

GUY DIDN'T HAVE horses anymore, but he kept rabbits in cages inside a room in his loose-planked old barn. In the same space were half a dozen ring-necked doves swooping past windows covered with wire mesh and coming to rest on shelves thick with feathers. Lulu could go right up to them and examine for as long as she liked the pencil line of pollen-yellow around each reddish-brown eye, the swatch of black on the back of the neck as if a guillotine had come down, the beautiful array of buffs and greys everywhere else.

At her side would be Sheba, the St. Bernard who leaned and leaned. Such a fine, flat, soft head and so unambiguous in her appetite for affection that she pressed her elephant-weight right into your side. Together they walked the snow-packed lane that wound past the barn and sheds and a section of sugar bush—out to the newer bungalow rented to a couple of schoolteachers—then back around to the original farmhouse where Lulu would live in her brother's absence. The night before, after checking out of her hotel while the others waited, she had followed them in her car, Nan and the tulips beside her, suitcases in the trunk. At seven in the morning Guy and Ducky had taken off for Toronto, and Lulu remained behind.

It was the end of March. The sap had been flowing in fits and starts for more than three weeks. If they were lucky, Guy had told her, it would flow for another one, even two weeks, before the leaves started to bud and the sap went cloudy and yellow.

That first morning she awakened to a robin singing—whistling up spring—and soon she was whistling up Sheba. They made a detour into the sugar bush, following Guy's snowmobile trail that crisscrossed the southeast-facing slope. In among the trees and out of the wind, she heard a slight rustling and tried to locate the source. Twigs rubbing against each other in the imperceptible breezes, or the last beech leaves working their way loose and falling on the snow, or the air itself. Save for the birds and these indeterminate sounds, it was silent in the woods.

She remembered being six years old and watching a pair of scruffy, whiskery men in red lumberjack shirts help her great-uncle gather the sap by horse and wagon, while patches of snow lingered on the uneven ground. She remembered leaning over the great long trough of simmering sap in the makeshift shanty and inhaling to the bottom of her lungs the steamy fumes so sweet and potent they caught in the back of her throat. She recalled arguing fiercely with Guy about the word "hundred," convinced it was hun*derd*. She didn't believe him for a second when he told her it was hun*dred*.

The ring-necked doves were cooing when she and Sheba entered the barn. Her brother's doves and rabbits were hobbies for Ducky's sake as much as his own. Lulu knelt down and lifted the smallest bunny out of its cage and stroked it with her gloved hand, while Sheba leaned in to lick its fur, motherly, protective, fascinated. It was peaceful here, yet there was so much life going on. Amid scratchings and the flutter of feathers, Lulu replenished the dishes of water and seeds and pellets, then stood a moment longer admiring how the birds sat close and puffed out their feathers to capture body heat and get by. Guy had assured her that he had never lost a bird to cold weather.

While she was having breakfast, Nan phoned her from her house down the road, a twenty-minute walk away, checking in as she would every day. Jim would be leaving the next morning for Boston, and then Nan too would be alone.

At nine o'clock the hired men showed up. Happily, unsurprisingly, one was Hugh Shapiro. The other was runny-nosed Junior, a high-school dropout from down the road. Lulu made them coffee, then at noon she joined them at the picnic table, shovelled free from its prison of snow beside the sugar shack, where they ate their sandwiches with the birds and the squirrels. By this time Junior felt so punk they told him to go home and stay there. Lulu would fill in as the hired hand. "Call me Slim," she said.

The original shanty was long gone, replaced by a solid sugar shack with narrow vents running the length of the roof. Stepping inside, she entered a workshop of a room, longer than wide, about twenty feet by fifteen, that smelled tangy and aromatic, of maple syrup and wood. Shafts of sunlight reached across to the giant wood-fired steel evaporator and the wall of stacked firewood on the left. A kitchen alcove on the right had a bank of four windows lighting up a countertop and sink and propane stove, and on the far side of the alcove a cubbyhole-office sheltered her great-uncle's rocking chair and a small desk and bookshelf. There she found Guy's dog-eared scribbler in which he tracked the progress of the sap harvest: the daily temperatures, the amount of syrup produced, the length of the run, the day the snow was gone, the day the ice went off the lake. Looking all around her, Lulu felt the same rush of happiness she had always felt backstage. Here too was the dim and dusky atmosphere of something creative going on that very few knew about.

That first day, when she turned into Slim, the sunshine disappeared by two in the afternoon, and half an hour later it began to snow, and snow so copiously and gently it was a wonder. Hugh remarked that on the open ground next to his house the snow now lay chest-deep. Record quantities, he said; an extraordinary winter. Snow was thigh-deep on his roof, waist-deep in the woods, chest-deep next to his house. In the sugar bush he and Guy had shovelled for a week to free up the blue tubing that ran from tree to tree, bringing the sap to the main pipeline that fed the holding tank on the shack's north side, where it stayed cool. Guy had scaled back from two thousand taps to five hundred. He was getting old, he'd told Lulu. All he wanted now was to work without quotas or pressures, keeping the tradition alive and not caring anymore if he broke even.

Earlier in the week, they had boiled about three hundred gallons of sap, getting thirty-one litres of syrup. Hugh would joke that when it came to measurements they were bilingual, moving back and forth between metric and imperial. "In that respect," he said, "we really are a bilingual country."

The next morning Lulu woke early out of a bad dream about showing up late and not knowing her lines. On her pillow she relaxed into the welcome reality of where she was: the warmth of the bed, the suggestion of daylight in the room, the sense of being on the verge of something new.

She dressed herself for outdoor work, and went downstairs to greet Sheba and make breakfast. Then she and the dog went out to visit the doves and rabbits, and then the sugar shack, where at 7 a.m. the thermometer beside the door read minus 3° C. For the sap to flow they needed temperatures of around plus 5° C by day and minus 5° C at night. Everything depended on the weather.

Inside, noting down the temperature and time in Guy's scribbler, Lulu felt as she did about Lanark before the fire, that an old-world sensibility might still exist if you were in the right place at the right time. From the windows above the sink, she watched the sun rise over the nearest island, spreading its pinks and yellows and golds. Her life had seen many more sunsets than sunrises and it was probably time to even the score.

Outside again, she went around the back to the holding tank, which rested on a wooden platform several feet above the ground. Curious to see how much sap had flowed in overnight, she climbed the four-rung ladder to look over the edge. Not much if any. It was less than a quarter full.

Hugh arrived at nine, as he had the day before. On this, the second day, sunshine swept down on them unimpeded, like Mongols on horseback, shocking the trees out of their torpor and Lulu too. Outside, her energy knew no bounds. She helped Hugh clear away several branches fallen across the lines of blue tubing, helped him check the lines for sagging and tightened them up, took note when he pointed out young maples bark-stripped by porcupines, and cedars nibbled by deer. By mid-morning it was plus 4° C and the sap was trickling into the holding tank. Hugh had her load up a toboggan with firewood from the open-sided woodshed (it shared a roof with the sugar shack) and pull it to the shack door, where she threw the wood inside and later topped up the pile extending across the front wall. Several trips, back and forth. The air off the snow was cool, the sun had real warmth, and the combination of warm and cool wove a spell.

A large part of the enchantment was Hugh. How had he ended up in this part of the world?

"I opened an atlas," he said.

He had been searching for a place called Killaloe, where friends of his were homesteading—draft dodgers, fellow hippies from California who had made a new life for themselves in Canada. They had invited him to come and stay after the

accident that shattered his leg and left him with his perma-
nent limp. In those days his bible was *Seven Years in Tibet* by the
mountaineer Heinrich Harrer and his favourite place to train
was Yosemite National Park. The summer he was twenty-
three, he told her, he was in the park with a pair of experienced
climbers, men in their forties. They were ahead of him, higher
up and tethered to each other, when he heard something fall.

"It sounded like a haul bag," he said. "Then I saw Joe
come into view and I heard Will scream. I saw Will next. They
fell a thousand feet."

"I suppose you can still hear that scream in your head,"
she said.

"You bet I can."

In scrambling back down the mountainside, he had mis-
judged a foothold and fallen thirty feet himself, breaking his
heel and ankle and knee. A dozen years later, he finally got
himself to Nepal, but only to see what he had missed out on.

"So you were looking for Killaloe," she reminded him.

"And I found it. Then I kept poring over the map of
Ontario and my finger suddenly hit Snow Road Station."
A smile creased his face. "I felt a little jolt of electricity under
my fingertip, a nice cool throb."

"Snow Road isn't on most maps," she said, sounding to
herself like an actor instructed by Beckett. No intonation.
No colour. A mild tone.

"You doubt me."

Lulu smiled too. Her show of resistance was like grabbing
a boy's hat and running off with it. "So what were you doing
back then when you weren't climbing mountains?"

He was working night shifts at a gas station. He had plenty of time to read and no one bothered him. "I was trying to write a novel," he said, "like half the world."

"And the woman who wrote the book about you?"

"Sylvia. She was thirty-one. A poet who turned into a pest."

"Before or after you ruined your leg?"

"We parted soon after," he said.

"I love the name too," Lulu said. "Snow Road Station. I always have."

2

THE NEXT DAY he gave her a chainsaw lesson, rigging her out in his safety goggles and leather gloves, plus Kevlar chaps to protect her thighs. "Like cowboy chaps," said Lulu, looking down at them with delight.

Safety was everything, he instructed. Never chainsaw when you're tired, never let your attention wander. The chain was going fifty miles an hour. "If one of these teeth," he fingered the chain, "catches on a twig, it can stop and kick back and throw you off balance." He showed her how to place her left hand, how to position her wrist, then oversaw her first attempt to chainsaw a log into pieces the right length for the evaporator's firebox, after which Lulu said into the restored silence, "Thanks, and I don't need to do it again."

"Okay."

"I don't need to climb every mountain and ford every stream."

"Right."

"I'll leave that to Nan."

"Nan," he said, and his voice betrayed his ongoing interest. He wanted to know how long they had been friends.

"A long time. We were at school together."

"And what was she like back then?"

"As a girl?" Thinking back, Lulu remembered dear Nan befriending her, rescuing her, the new girl in class, and wondered if anything was more heaven-sent than a true friend. "She was kind and smart and on her own."

Her thoughtful eyes gravitated to the flock of redpolls at the birdfeeder near the picnic table—so small, with vivid patches of red on top of their heads.

"Spring brings out their colours," Hugh said, observing them too. "Especially against the white snow. Although, 'white snow'—that's a misconception. If you look at a white fence half-buried in a snowdrift, you see it looks yellow. Snow is blue."

She really did like him.

"So why do you admire Nan so much?" she said.

"You must know. She's your friend."

"But say it."

Looking off at the trees, he replied, "Her self-sufficiency. Her willingness to make her way in the world. Her honesty." He said, "But you have that too. Self-sufficiency."

"You do know she has terrible taste in men."

"I know she made one bad choice."

"She made two terrible marriages." Then ashamed of her grudging remark, "Not terrible taste. Terrible luck."

Hugh nodded.

"So tell me about you and Julie," she said. "My brother's wife."

"Nothing to tell."

Lulu gave him a long look. "How would you like to have your nose punched the other way?"

That made him laugh, but his answer was calm and sober. "Julie's unhappy in her marriage, but Guy is a friend of mine. Come on, Slim," he smiled. "Help me stack this wood."

Soon the sun on the snow was so bright she turned away to shield her eyes, only to feel its heat on her back, and with one hot stroke an avalanche of ugliness hit her broadside. She sat down heavily on the nearest upturned log.

"Tired?" Hugh said from behind her.

Everything inside her had lurched sideways, inside the bad old girl who had made a younger woman very happy, then flirted with an asshole and ended up in a ditch. She remembered Tony, remembered years ago at a party someone mentioning Tony Lloyd and his girlfriend walking down the railway tracks in the rain, looking like the ragged end of nowhere. That was me, she had almost said. Then and now.

"I'm fine." Getting to her feet. "Now you'll show me how to use an axe."

Taking up a wide stance, as Hugh instructed, glancing overhead to make sure there were no obstacles in the way, holding the axe handle low, a few inches from the base so the blade would hit the ground and not her leg if she missed, she raised the axe high, and thinking of Barbara Stanwyck saying she needed that man like the axe needs the turkey, she brought it down on John Sharpe's head.

That night and the next day, the sap kept flowing. The weather was perfect, ranging from minus 9° C to plus 5° C. By the following day, with the holding tank two-thirds full—about four hundred gallons of sap—they had enough on hand to boil. Now Lulu would remember afresh how much work went into a bottle of maple syrup.

Every fifteen minutes or so you had to feed the fire. Hugh set the timer on his watch and the moment it dinged, he drew on Guy's battered motorcycle gloves that reached high on his arms, grabbed four logs from the pile against the near wall and dumped them on the floor next to the firebox's double doors; then on his knees he unlatched the left door, threw the logs in fast so as not to let the heat escape, and closed the door tight. Fifteen minutes later, he fed the other half of the firebox. In the intervals, walking Lulu through each step, he checked the valves controlling the inflow of sap from the holding tank into the evaporator's back pan, and kept his eye on its passage into the partitioned front pan. For just as you need an even flame, you need a constant level of sap. The old adage about a watched pot was true, but so was the non-adage about an unwatched pot: walk away and you'll come back to the scorched smell of burnt marshmallows and a blackened bubbling mess.

Under ideal conditions, he said, you could get sap to syrup in six hours. But conditions were never ideal. The wood wasn't right, the fire burned too fast or too slow, the weather was too humid. Seasoned maple was the right kind of wood.

A strong-blowing wind that pulled the steam up out of the vents and blew it away—that was the right kind of wind. Usually, it took eight to ten hours to boil down a few hundred gallons of sap.

Soon it was Lulu who was stoking the fire, while Hugh brought in more wood or did the fussy work of sterilizing bottles in a big pot on the propane stove. In the fifteen-minute interludes, she moved in a circle around the stainless-steel evaporator, checking the sap level, checking the temperature, being careful not to burn herself on the hot metal. By the afternoon Hugh was remarking on her patience and energy. She replied that actors were good at both. "Or maybe not good," she said, "but we do a lot of waiting, and we're good at working. We work hard when we have work."

The bane of her life had been the lulls between jobs. Over the years she had grabbed anything that came along—coaching, combat training, voice-overs, audiobooks, commercials, movies-of-the-week, bit parts on television nothing was beneath her. All the aging actors she knew were the same, forever asking themselves when was the next job going to materialize, why wasn't the work coming, why were *they* getting work when I'm the better actor. Hounded by insecurity and financial stress. So in the end most of them threw in the towel. Became teachers or directors or therapists or carpenters or cooks or priests. Those who stuck it out sometimes had a late success, landing an enviable role, and Lulu would go to the performance and wonder why it wasn't better. Like Nan, she thought, coming to see her in whatever-play-it-was and sliding away at the end. *An actor who would never be great.*

Hugh startled her by saying, "Guy told me what happened with your play." He was half-hidden by the curtain of steam rising from the boiling sap.

Okay. She thought he might have. "What did he say?"

"The theatre screwed you over."

Her loyal brother. "That was part of it," she agreed, letting her suspicions come to the fore. "I think the director wanted to get rid of me."

She had stripped down to her flannel shirt by this time and her forehead was damp with sticky steam and sweat. "I mean, the fact they were able to find someone over the weekend to finish the run. He must have contacted Olivia ahead of time. 'Would you be willing to do this?'" Imitating Richard's curt and peevish voice. "And then there was my own self-sabotage. I was blanking on my lines, I didn't tell them where I was."

She paused, sick at heart, and Hugh asked if she had never forgotten her lines before.

"A few times. But I improvised my way out of it. This was different. It was terrifying, like falling from an enormous height. Like your mountain-climbing friends."

He nodded. "It's a long way down."

"It felt like game over." She grappled with her shirt and twisted it. "You lose all your confidence," she said.

"Confidence comes back," he said. "With time."

"I don't know. It doesn't feel like it will." Lulu turned away. "Anyway, it was also pretty fucking convenient—Olivia showing up like that. I'm too emotional," she muttered. "But it hurts."

She took the long-handled skimmer with its perforated bottom and concentrated on removing the froth from the boiling sap in the back pan. Greyish-white foam that she shook and knocked into a plastic pail. She dipped the skimmer into another pail of water to clean it. Then she was stoking the fire again.

It was the transformation that made her marvel. The progression from colourless sap with the slightest trace of sweetness and the faintest of odours (like newly fallen leaves) to liquid ambrosia.

From a stool positioned next to the temperature gauge at the end of the evaporator, Hugh called out the numbers: 6.7, 6.8, 6.9. The sap-on-its-way-to-syrup had been snaking its way through each of the six divisions in the big partitioned front pan, pushed along by the raw sap flowing in. As it progressed, it sweetened and darkened. The magic number was seven. at seven degrees above the boiling point of water, the sap had the density of syrup and was ready to draw off.

Hugh opened the spigot, and Lulu squatted on her heels and watched piping-hot syrup the colour of amber pour into a bucket lined with cone-shaped filters of orlon and felt. She was aware of Hugh's capable hands and her own roughened fingers, her overwarm armpits, her creaking knees. As soon as the gauge dropped below seven, he turned off the tap. Not until they got it back up to the magic number could they draw off another batch.

At the counter Hugh spooned syrup into a cup for them to taste, urging her to sniff it first, like a fine wine. Lulu inhaled, and her head went into raptures. Then she closed her eyes to concentrate on the flavour.

"Pure maple," she said. "Delicate at first and then powerful. Smooth. Sweet. A little smoky. Wow."

She opened her eyes and her broad smile met his. "It's like a jazz trumpeter playing a bunch of notes," she said. "The taste goes on and on."

3

THE FIRST TIME they boiled they didn't finish until after
dark, stoking up the fire to get three more run-offs, spaced
about an hour apart, for a total of twenty-nine litres of syrup.

Hugh stayed on to guide her through the post-boil rou-
tine: washing the reusable filters with hot water but no soap;
leaving enough sap in the evaporator pans so they wouldn't
scorch as the fire cooled; shutting the vents in the roof;
then double-checking that the valve from the holding tank
was closed, so they wouldn't have sap all over the floor in
the morning.

Afterwards, she toppled into bed and slept the kind of
dead-to-the-world sleep she hadn't known since childhood.
At first light she was wide awake, as if it were Christmas
morning, eager to discover how much sap had flowed in overnight. All her muscles ached, yet even before making coffee

she and Sheba were on their way to the sugar shack. Using a headlamp, she climbed the ladder to the holding tank and got a reading on the measuring stick. Eight inches. One inch was twenty-five gallons. So that was two hundred. They needed at least another hundred before they could boil again.

That morning she scoured the evaporator's big front pan with a cloth and hot water, getting rid of the sugar-sand that had built up as the sap thickened into syrup, and while she worked she questioned Hugh about how he managed to make a living. He turned his hand to whatever needed doing: fence building and repair in the summer, piano tuning generally in the fall and spring, clearing snow off cottage rooftops in the winter. He had done well that year, making 175 bucks for every cleared roof. And people were grateful since all over eastern Ontario and Quebec roofs were collapsing.

She began to wonder if she too could make a living here. Nan had her bookkeeping job at the township offices, driving into Lanark three mornings a week, but then Nan actually understood tax rolls and accounting. Like Hugh, she had skills that fitted her for the real world.

"And you live here year-round without losing your mind?" she said.

"Oh, I go to New York twice a year. That keeps me on a level. And then I'm happy to come home again."

"Where you have your widows," she said. And not expecting a serious answer, "What is it with widows?"

He replied without missing a beat, "Their husbands die and they blossom. Like Nan. I've seen it time and time again."

All morning the sap trickled in, then around noon it stopped for no immediately apparent reason. But it was in the nature of sap to behave in ways that nobody could predict. They lunched on sandwiches in Guy's kitchen, and in the early afternoon Hugh went out with his chainsaw to get ahead of the perpetual need for firewood. Mainly, they relied on dead or dying trees and downed limbs. Lulu followed with the toboggan, Sheba at her heels. Whatever Hugh cut up, Lulu ferried back to the woodshed. Soon they were so warm from their exertions they had to peel down to their long-sleeved undershirts.

A pair of nuthatches kept them company along with several chickadees flitting about. Hugh pointed out trails no wider than a stitched seam where deer came to drink at the tumbling creek. He spotted coyote tracks, narrower and more oval than a dog's, then drew her attention to the six wild turkeys coming down the lane. Big, glossy, black-and-bronze iridescent birds, they mounted a snowbank and reached up for the sumac tassels and their burgundy berries. He drew in his breath, "It's like a Riopelle. His colours exactly."

Nice, she thought, and her sense of him opened wide, a window on the first warm day of spring. She recalled what she had seen of his own paintings the night she ended up on his doorstep, when he had been so kind and when she discovered that his landscapes weren't mediocre at all.

In the V of his undershirt, his soft chest hairs were damp with perspiration. She wanted nothing more than to reach out and stroke them.

That night she lay awake for a long time. When at last she slept, she dreamt she was seated on a near-empty stage. A man announced that she had won an award, but he called her Lula Blakey. She shot her arm emphatically into the air: "Pronounce my name right! Pronounce my name right or I won't accept the award!" Then she was in an empty theatre where they couldn't sell a single ticket because she had confessed in an interview that she used homeopathy.

Apparently, her unconscious mind hadn't caught up with her decision to leave acting behind. Maybe it never would. She was very aware that she had nothing on the horizon: no work, no plan, no income except for the rent from her flat in Montreal.

For the second time during that first week, she put on her brother's cross-country skis and went out early with Sheba on the snowmobile trails through the bush. A skiff of fresh snow and her mind evened out and the dream-riddled night fell away. What ease of movement over the white and under the blue. Off to the side broken twigs had left imprints in the softening snow. Looking straight down into one well of blue light, she saw the black twig at the bottom and remembered Eldon, her set-designing pal, dear Eldon, telling her about a turning point in his life. How he had been sitting on a rock beside a lake, alone and desolate, when he noticed insects skittering across the surface of the water. Then fish moving under the water. Then weeds moving under the fish. The weeds reminded him of winter grasses bent over by drifting snow. Then a footstep in the woods—the crackle of leaves—connected him to even more hidden life. And he realized he was part of an orchestration of movement that had no end.

The twig beneath the snow—the snow traced with shadows—the shadows pockmarked by more snow dropping like soft apples from boughs overhead—and the great blueness above.

On these early morning outings, she had moments now and again of self-forgetfulness similar to what sometimes graced her on stage, when she wasn't thinking ahead or thinking back, she was living the life of her character, utterly present with the other actors and with the audience. Now her role was something else entirely. It was paying attention to all the life around her that wasn't paying the least regard to her.

A cold wave stopped the sap in its tracks for a day and a night. Then on a sunny afternoon the trees facing south started to run, and once again Lulu marvelled at what they gave. As the days got warmer, the syrup became progressively darker and in her opinion more delicious. Fuller-bodied, stronger in flavour.

"I wonder if *I* could live here," she said to Hugh.

His reply was slow in coming. "You're an actor," he pointed out, his face noncommittal. "I have a good life here, but it's a small life, a reduced life."

"A reduced life." She considered his words.

"You're a big personality," he said. "This is no place for you."

"I don't know." She glanced around and remembered her great-uncle's gnarled, capable, generous hands. "You can spread yourself thin or you can go deep." She swept her hand in a circle to include their whole operation. "Reduce gallons of sap and you get syrup. Forty parts to one."

Hugh threw her an appreciative look, only to say a moment later, "But the point I take from that is you need the forty gallons first." He looked her in the eye. "I guess you've gathered your forty gallons? I'm not sure I have. I never took advantage of all there was." His tired eyes were regretful, not bitter. "And yet I'm very satisfied with where I am right now."

"So am I," Lulu said. "So am I."

4

ON THE DAYS when she and Hugh weren't boiling, Lulu lent Nan a hand with her sap gathering and syrup making.

Her brother had called to say he would stay on in Toronto for another few days. He was looking up old friends and seeing Ducky, meeting her after school and walking her home. "It's hard to keep up with her," he had said, proud and wistful.

Turning in at Nan's, she spied her moving among the trees and thought again that Nan was something of a tree herself: aging, erect, full of life. She called out to her and Nan shouted back that the sap was "pouring!" Her voice was croaky and ecstatic, her face tanned from sunshine and smoke.

Together they emptied the Dominion & Grimm sap buckets from Nan's twenty tapped trees into the five-gallon pail that rode on a toboggan, then pulled the toboggan down and around and over to the woodstove, where they lifted the pail and emptied it into the blue barrel. Four trips in all, and their take was almost fifteen gallons of sap.

Nan had no goal beyond supplying her own needs. Her method was simple. She followed a relaxed schedule of feeding the fire every twenty minutes or so, rather than every fifteen. At the same time she ladled warming sap from the back pan into what was boiling briskly in the front pan, keeping the level constant. Then she topped up the back pan with sap from the barrel. On the days she boiled, she kept this up from dawn to dusk, using up the whole of that day's and the previous day's take. Sap was highly perishable, like milk; the best syrup, the most flavourful, came from the freshest sap. During the twenty-minute intervals, Nan liked to sit in her outdoor chair and read, or snooze in the sun, or practise a song on the button accordion she was learning how to play, or listen on her battery-powered transistor to Valley Heritage Radio out of Renfrew. "Where else," she said, "can you hear, one after the other, Johnny Cash, Diana Ross, a gospel song, and a fiddle tune?"

With only twenty trees, Nan could manage on her own, although usually she had help from willing friends or family, like Jim, Ducky, Guy, and now Lulu. Using heavy work gloves, Nan emptied the syrup into a big soup pot, which Lulu carried inside to the kitchen stove, and there they brought it back to a brisk boil before pouring it through a filter-lined colander placed over a saucepan. Left behind in the filter were the sugar-sand and dark motes of this and that: bark, bugs, moths, ashes, grit. They poured the saucepan of pure hot syrup through a kitchen funnel into an unwashed liquor bottle kept sterile by the splash of liquor at the bottom. A tip from Nan's late brother: liquor bottles spared you the time and trouble of sterilizing jars.

On this particular day, once they were outside again by the woodstove, Lulu asked Nan if she still had feelings for her brother, for Guy.

The colour rose in Nan's face. "I'm not looking for romance," she said.

"Why not?"

"Especially with someone who's been married three times and has one affair after another." She dug the toe of her boot into the melting snow and rubbed the bridge of her nose.

"He's in love with you, you know. He always has been."

"How do you know?"

"He told me at the wedding."

"Well," Nan said, "he hasn't told me." She cocked her head. "You're playing matchmaker, Lu. But you're the one who wants love in her life."

"Don't you?"

"I have it," Nan said. "I'm in love with this place."

Sometimes Hugh Shapiro also dropped by to see if Nan needed anything, which meant the three of them would sit around in Nan's camp and discuss the fine art of sugaring. What really set the sap running, the two veterans agreed, was sunshine: hang the buckets on the south side of the trees, and if nothing blocks the flood of light, the sap just pours. They also agreed that the sweetness of the sap varied from year to year. "It's a little dilute this year," Nan said. "2008."

They were a good fit, Lulu could see that, Hugh from else-where and Nan having lived all those years in New York, and both of them able to do all manner of things.

"One year," Hugh was saying, "was it 1990? I remember the sap poured out for a week solid. I was helping a friend of mine and we used everything he had to hold it, even his aluminum canoes."

Nan's delighted reaction—her wonderful wide smile—was infectious and Lulu was struck anew by her outdoor radiance, her lively eyes, her long-fingered elegant hands. She was a practical woman with a poetic bent, now saying, "The trees are very sensitive in a way we don't yet understand. You need the contrast between cold nights and warmer days for the sap to flow, but the edges of the contrast are mysterious. That's why it's so hard to predict."

Lulu had to ask, "And drilling into them and robbing their sap doesn't shorten their lives? Guy swears it doesn't, but I have to wonder."

Nan assured her the tap-holes were like paper cuts in your finger. They healed over. And during drought years she did not tap. "Generally," she said, "the trees stay open for about six weeks. This season we'll be lucky to get five."

"A six-week run," Lulu said. Looking around her, she recalled her old idea of staging "Hansel and Gretel" in a sugar bush. "You'd have the sugar house," she said, "you'd make taffy on the snow, you'd shove the witch into a vat of boiling sap. I had it all figured out. A three-week run during maple-syrup time."

"Children would come in droves," laughed Nan. "Bus-loads of schoolchildren. The road would be clogged with pay-ing customers."

"It's a great idea," Hugh said. "You could still do it."

"Oh, it would take a lot of doing," Lulu said.

Still, with every passing hour she felt fitter, stronger, clearer in her head, as if she were ironing out the many kinks in her life.

Rain came towards the end of that first week of April. This wasn't the unseasonable rain of mid-March that thaws the trees and the ground and gets the sap flowing, but the warmer rain that brings trees into bud and the syrup season to an end.

Waiting for the rain to let up, Lulu and Hugh retired to Guy's living room with Sheba, and snoozed or read. A dozen Scandinavian thrillers were on Guy's shelves and she settled in with Henning Mankell, becoming absorbed in Kurt Wallander's failed ambitions and failing memory. Hunger drove her to the kitchen cupboards, where she found a bag of stale pistachios and freshened them up in the oven before setting them out in a bowl. "I love warm nuts," she said, offering the bowl to Hugh.

He put his finger on his page and leaned back with a smile. "Oh, I can keep you supplied," he said.

Whereupon she took him by the hand and led him upstairs to her bedroom. The weight of their clothes tipped over the chair, but she didn't care about that.

The next morning she woke up, still smiling, to the patter of ice pellets on the window. That day it rained again. In the woods the snow cover was still complete, although in the hollows water was rising through the snow. The sap was running well, despite overnight temperatures not much below freezing. She and Hugh boiled again, getting another twenty-six litres of syrup, after which they rewarded themselves by tumbling back into Lulu's bed.

They were having spring sunsets now. Colours not seen all winter reappeared in the sky—shades of pink that floated high and loose like Easter hats, like flowers. At dawn the snow was faint-pink as the sun rose, and the woods themselves were light-filled, yet full of long shadows and air in subtle motion. Lulu, in her heavy boots, met pockets of air that were strangely warm, as if she were swimming between warm spots and cool spots in a lake. Hemlock needles dusted the surface of the snow, as did beech leaves whitened by winter winds and only now letting go. Even when overcast, the woods were bright. It was like being inside an opal.

Then she was at Nan's again, where in exposed and sunny places the surface snow was worked into fine patterns, like weathered leaves on the forest floor. She was skimming froth from the bubbling sap and breathing in the smoky fumes, saturating herself with sweet vapours and turning *as brown in hue / As hazel-nuts, and sweeter than the kernels*. Ah, Shakespeare. Night after night her hands made a woodsy sachet under her nose that drew her into effortless sleep.

"What is it?" Nan said. "You can't keep a smile off your face."

"You may not want to hear this," Lulu laughed a wicked belly laugh, "but I've been having the most terrific sex."

5

THEY WERE HEARING loons now and mallard ducks and the soft cackling of wood frogs. The ice on the lake of bays had gone mauve, almost black, and channels of water were pushing it apart. Soon trout lilies would be coming up around the back door. Wild leeks would follow and butterflies.

End of the season, Lulu thought. End of the run. She helped Nan finish the last batch of the year, heating the remaining saucepan of near-syrup on the kitchen stove, filtering and bottling it, then adding the final bottle to the stash of nineteen on Nan's pantry shelves.

"Nan, if you don't need me, I'll mosey on down the road."

She couldn't put it off any longer—the Montreal part of her life. Guy was back from Toronto and it was time to tackle the future: extend the sublet of her apartment if she was going to do that, move back in if she wasn't; talk to Equity and her agent; make sure she was paid for her final week of *Happy Days*. And so on.

Hugh Shapiro had offered to go with her. They would have a holiday together in Montreal. Maybe drive into the Laurentians. Rent a chalet for a few days.

"You're lovely," she had said to him, managing to convey flattery and discouragement at the same time.

She could see the mute surprise in his face. Her answer rather surprised her too. But she didn't have the energy for anything save the tasks ahead, the decisions she had to make, the embarrassments she had to face. "Keep a spot on your dance card open," she teased, "for a babe among your widows."

Now Nan was asking her, "Do you have to go?"

She felt she did. But how she loved the quiet and the sounds—of rain, crows, breezes in the trees, the subdued restlessness of the weather. "What do crows eat?" she wondered aloud.

"They're omnivores. And they never forget a face. Or so I've read."

"You mean a human face?"

"They'll remember you when you come back. 'Where have you been, Lulu? We missed you.'" Nan said, "You'll be back in the summer?"

"Sooner, I expect."

"Hugh," Nan said with a smile.

And reassured by her benign good humour, Lulu said, "You're not pissed off at me?"

"For what?"

"Getting there first, I guess."

"Oh, Lu. I'm not like you when it comes to sex. I don't have your confidence, or your energy. I marvel at it, to be honest. You amaze me."

"But he had his eye on you, not me."

"He has his eye on a lot of women." Nan went over to her pantry and came back with a bourbon bottle of maple syrup. "Take this along with you," she said, putting it into Lulu's hands.

"So you think he's feckless?"

"Not feckless. Not unreliable either. He's a very nice guy. Reliably available, I'd say."

They went out to Lulu's car. Lulu opened the trunk and there was the black plastic bag she had failed to dispose of. "Garbage," she muttered of the coat rotting in a foul man's pee, shoving it into the corner and vowing to dump it the first chance she got. She stowed the maple syrup in the space between suitcases.

A car turned into the lane. They paused and watched it approach. Blake parked beside them and got out, bareheaded, wearing a leather jacket that blew wide in the wind.

"You're still here," he said to Lulu.

"I'm on my way, as you see."

But Nan put a hand on her arm, so Lulu allowed herself to go back inside with Nan and her troubled son.

In the kitchen Nan asked him if he was hungry. "I'm angry," Blake said, hanging his jacket by the door.

"At me," Nan said.

"At myself," he said.

Lulu went to the sink, where the dishes from lunch were stacked, and began to wash up.

Nan pulled out a chair at the table and sat down. "Tell me," she said.

Blake put his hands on his chest. "Religion used to fill this void in me, but I went too far with it. It was my life. It was all I had." He said, "I'm angry that I had no faith in *myself*."

"Sit down," his mother said softly.

He swung a chair out from the table and straddled it, then levelled his mother with his gaze. "I want to be a strong person in charge of my own life and I'm not."

"You're strong," Nan said. "You're terrifying."

He shook his head with disgust. "I'm all wrapped up in myself."

Lulu left the sink and joined them at the table, taking a chair at one end. From the window she watched crows winging overhead—clearing the sky of everything but low-lying clouds. She understood how crows might be omnivores, but what did they survive on in the winter?

"You're about to be a father," Nan reminded her son. "Being a parent stirs up so much. All the old hurts and confusions."

He raised his eyes. "I know. I've been thinking a lot about my childhood."

Nan nodded warily. "Yes?"

He opened his mouth to speak, then attacked the wedding band on his finger, shoved it back and forth and said nothing.

Lulu was struck by his pallor and intensity, and by the quality of Nan's attention. It was all you needed for a play, she thought. A table and a chair, the changing light. The moment when someone could go one way or another.

"Let it out," Nan told him.

"Jim always came first," he said.

That stopped her. "Not always," Nan said finally. "Not ever." She reminded him, "There's eight years between you. Until he came along you were everything to me."

"I don't remember that," he said.

"I know. You've told me."

"*Why* don't I remember?"

Lulu leaned forward, "Try harder," she said. But they didn't appear to be listening. This was only between them: a long, sad, intricate history.

Nan said, "John made it difficult between us. I'm not blaming him. Or I guess I am."

"He was better when you weren't around."

"Why?" Stung and mystified.

"I don't know why. But he was."

They really were alike, Lulu thought. The bony contours of their faces, their self-denying bent. Nan on her quiet warpath to do without. Blake on his fundamentalist path, but wanting off now and not knowing where to go.

He got to his feet and went over to the window. It had begun to rain without them noticing. He turned and said to his mother, "I'm not as important to you as you are to me."

Nan swallowed. "It's never been exactly obvious that I'm important to you." She paused. "I think about you *all* the time. You're on my mind *all* the time."

He stared at the floor and Nan's eyes swung to Lulu for help.

What could she say except what she was thinking? That acting had been *her* religion, filling the emptiness in her. So she sympathized, she told Blake. They were in the same boat.

His head jerked up. "Only I quit and you got fired."

Lulu burst out laughing. And in the face of her merriment, he relented, he smiled. "Sorry," he said.

"Like father, like son. Guy used to always get in the first punch too," she said. "So why did you give up preaching?"

He ran his hands through his limp hair. "I couldn't do it anymore. I don't know why."

"Sure you do."

He shook his head. "I just felt fake."

"Oh, honey, I know how you feel. It's the worst feeling. I'd do anything not to feel it." Lulu studied him for a moment. "I'm on a different track now. I want to be more like your mother. Have a life more like hers."

He shot her a look of surprise and so did Nan. Surprise, disbelief. "It's true," Lulu said to them. Nan knew who she was; she didn't need applause. Knowing who you are and being fine with that—Jim's words echoed in her head. "Except, of course, I want more laughs and more sex."

"I just want to start over," Blake said.

Nan broke in. "But you'll keep your teaching job. You have a wife. Soon you'll have a child."

"Do I need reminding?"

Silence.

Lulu asked, "When is the baby due?"

"End of July," he said.

In four months, then, more or less.

"Blake," his mother said, "having responsibilities is good. It gives you a purpose. It gives you people to look after and care about."

Blake went to the sink and poured himself a glass of water. Setting it down half-empty, he turned to them.

"And if I don't love Bethany?"

More silence.

"But you'll love the child," Nan said, "and the child will love you both."

6

LULU'S STREET IN downtown Montreal was rue Fabre. Michel Tremblay had grown up at one end and Maureen Forrester at the other, so Lulu liked to think of herself as bookended by the living playwright and the late contralto. It was barely spring in the Plateau. Soon, however, the trees would leaf out and her neighbours on either side would leaf out too, moving onto their balconies, cooking on their barbecues, partying with free-wheeling gusto.

She owned her third-floor apartment (in the Quebec style, an outdoor stairway led to the second floor and then an indoor stairway to the third), having bought it with the money left to her in her mother's will, over time reconciling herself to Guy's behind-the-scenes machinations which secured the property at the lake for himself. After all, he then helped her buy the apartment, a backwoods Anglo braving Quebec for her sake, discovering he liked everyone he met and rather changing his mind about those dirty separatists. How many actors owned their own lodgings? Precious few.

During her stint in Ottawa, she had rented the two-bedroom flat to a couple of actors, only one of whom was still there, Adèle, a toothy blonde worried about being over the hill though she wasn't yet thirty. At first, Lulu kept silent about being fired, but Adèle already knew, as was evident from her skittish questions and oh-my-God reactions of pretend shock.

What swam into Lulu's mind was the memory of an older actor she had admired named Margot Lennox. Years ago in Toronto Margot was auditioning for a new play and Lulu was one of the readers. Margot would have been in her late fifties by then and she wasn't getting much work anymore. In the audition she was impressive, going deep into her part where only the best actors go. At one point she asked how a name was pronounced. Was it ouch and such? And the young playwright, apparently not certain himself, said, "Sure, that'll do." Then Margot, with a flick of professional impatience, said to him, "Well, it's not Margotte. Which way is it?" Out of the corner of her eye, Lulu saw the director clock the edge in her voice, and as soon as she left he said, "Well, you know, I've heard she's difficult to work with. She has problems with booze. She was here more than an hour in advance." As if being early were a strike against her. And what Lulu remembered was threefold: her dismay that this talented older woman was being so casually cast aside; her disappointment in herself for not defending her; and her quickening sense, even then, that she was probably headed for Margot's fate.

=

The next morning Lulu stood at her front window, looking down at rue Fabre. She had left a message for Stanley, her mouthy, slippery, silver-haired agent, and was waiting to see if he would call back. Stanley Drake had been her agent for fifteen years. She tended to say he was less than useless, knowing his opinion of her was no more flattering. But over the years he had been helpful too, once telling her to give the self-denigrating voice in her head a name. She had come up with "Gertrude Bumfuck," after which Gertrude B. was a running joke between them.

"Lulu! You're still alive. Where have you been?"

"I'm sorry," she said.

He paused to shout a goodbye to someone, then in his gravelly voice, "I just spoke with accounting. They've got your cheque."

"I didn't do anything wrong," Lulu said.

"I believe you, sweetheart."

"It was a little fuck-up. I didn't sign out." She paused. "But they're supposed to tell you beforehand about extra rehearsals." Hearing her meagre excuses, she despised herself. "That's spelled out in the contract . . ."

"So you're pursuing wrongful dismissal?"

Silence.

Then she sighed. "I'm a mess, to tell you the truth. I kept blanking on my lines."

"Well, the torture's over," he said. "Don't beat yourself up too much. Don't let this get into your head."

Still looking down at the street, half listening to Stanley tell her it was a hard industry and not to lose hope—his standard line—she recognized the young woman in gym clothes pushing her bicycle along the sidewalk. They had bonded one day over the historic plaque in front of Maureen Forrester's childhood home, when the young woman told her she had been listening to *Desert Island Discs* that very morning and Colin Firth had chosen Forrester singing Mahler as one of his picks. Apparently, he had learned about her at drama school when his Canadian roommate put on a recording of a voice so haunting and gorgeous, he had asked, "Who's *that*?" And his roommate replied, "That's my Mom."

Hearing the punchline, which was so unexpected, Lulu's eyes had welled up. Partly, it was the surprise connection between a mother and son. The rest was knowing what happened to that marvellous voice, how after rising out of near-poverty on this very street to a stellar career and a well-earned reputation as a feisty, funny, generous national treasure, rather like the massive elm tree in Snow Road Station, Forrester had slid downhill into alcoholism, dementia, penury.

Stanley was still talking. "We knew going in it was going to be tough. Richard's a prick. He's always been a prick. We'll avoid the Richards out there and only deal with fun people from now on."

"Stanley, listen to me. I can't do it anymore."

Silence at his end. Then he said, "Take your time, sweetheart. Don't do anything rash."

She heard him cough into his hand and imagined him checking his watch. An agent in his seventies. He knows our

vagaries, she thought, he's been privy to so much disappointment. He wasn't going to be an emotional companion through
this last act of her life, but then that wasn't his job.

Lulu watched spring fully arrive and the parks fill up with sun-
bathers, Frisbee-throwers, picnickers, dog walkers, cyclists:
city life. She remembered the shock of returning to Canada
after a dozen years of scrounging a living in New York and
Mexico and seeing fresh snow in late March and April, and
even, God help her, the beginning of May. Snow in the air
and snow on the ground, and her mother ill and dying at the
lake. That first winter, whenever she got away from Snow
Road to Montreal and her rented room, she would take her
skis and a flask of gin to the moonlit paths on Mount Royal,
and despite her worries she was happy. In late May her mother
had died and in the summer—that fraught summer of 1995
leading up to Quebec's second referendum on independence—
she rediscovered Nan. Their only flaring disagreement had
been over Nan's visceral Canadian nationalism, so at odds
with Lulu's firm sympathies for Quebec's restless energy—its
desire to assert itself, remake itself, be its own country. But
she knew more now than she did then, more of Nan's personal
history, the old hurts and fears she had kept under wraps.

Montreal had both history and beauty, centuries of it.
Lulu felt closer here to her mother the Irish-Quebecer, who
at eighteen had married a moody, volatile guy from Ontario
and followed him to Seattle, then the Yukon, then Ottawa,
and finally Snow Road Station. Like her mother, Lulu spoke
French, and not badly either. But she had learned that the

Québécois family of actors was a very tight clan, and she had never managed to get more than small parts in plays and occasional movies, usually if they needed someone who spoke French with an American or an English accent, or if they needed someone who didn't speak at all.

Now on her long walks through the city during this late spring of 2008, she passed the theatre school Ducky would be attending in the fall. During the half-dozen summers of her theatre camp on Guy's farm, there had been only one child who could act. The others had learned their lines with dazzling speed, but Ducky was the lightning bolt. And how she worked! As dedicated as a farmhand bringing in the harvest. Even at thirteen, she was a little professional. A pro.

Thinking these thoughts, Lulu remembered Sal, the stage manager, moving her to tears one day by speaking out on behalf of actors, saying it takes a lot out of you to become a transparent vessel for the playwright. You have to be so brave to subject yourself to three and a half weeks of criticism, constantly getting bits of your skin flayed off. Okay, but try it this way. No, that's not working either. Actors are enormously disciplined in the rehearsal hall, Sal had said, bucking her up with encouragement and appeals to her self-respect. "You are, Lu. You're great and it's coming together." It did come together—in its way and for a while—before it all went south.

One afternoon, passing the Café Cherrier with its wraparound terrace, a favourite spot, she crossed St. Louis Square to the cobblestoned street that led towards the student ghetto and

McGill University, eventually passing the used bookstore run by thin Adrian, who rarely smiled but had efficiently tracked down for her the biography of Samuel Beckett, a century ago it seemed. She entered the campus under a sprinkling of rain, wondering if any of the students might be Tony Lloyd's sleek and spoilt brat.

The extensive lawns were greening up, the trees were filmy with new buds. In the distance magnolias with big white blossoms drew her to their sheltered spot.

Some of the flowers were still unfurling from their fat, furry, silvery buds. Others were wide open, spilling into the air a licorice-and-lemon fragrance that knocked her flat. She found a bench nearby as the sun came out and in its gentle warmth everything around her came to life. And so did she. All that was wrong could be set right. She would use her apartment as rental income; she would ask her brother about renting his bungalow after his tenants moved out in June; she would make a new life for herself in Snow Road Station.

"Lulu!"

And this time she knew without being told. Raising her hands in mock horror, "Aren't you supposed to be in Bangkok?"

Tony sank down beside her and the bench sank too. "You almost missed me," he said. "I leave tomorrow." Giving her a genial once-over, "How are you, Lu?"

"Apart from getting fired, never better."

His belly laugh came with an offer of help. If she needed money, say the word.

"My rich ex-boyfriend." She wouldn't have minded hearing him confess that leaving her was the biggest mistake of his life; every morning he drank a vat of tears. "So where do you stay when you're here in Montreal?"

"I have a friend . . ."

"Mabel," she said. "Your friend Mabel."

His laugh again. And the sun so warm on the side of her face.

"I'm moving to Snow Road," she told him.

"That's not you," he said.

She didn't have to ask why not because he told her, putting his hands on either side of her knee and leaning close, "You're a city girl, Lu. Snow Road is a dead end."

"It's not dead," she replied. "There's nothing dead about it."

He searched her face. "You've met someone."

She smiled.

"The piano player?"

She had to laugh. He had always known who attracted her, sometimes before she knew it herself. And sure, having Hugh in Snow Road urging her to come back didn't hurt.

"You're an actress, Lu. You need an audience."

"Not anymore."

"I remember how ambitious you were. Acting came first. It was life and death."

"You left *me*," she laughed.

He grinned and kept going, and she wasn't averse to hearing about herself all those years ago. "I remember you in rooming houses," he said, "being fed by your actor friends. Making lists of all the parts you were going to play." He said, "I remember the great reviews you got."

"For a while," she said.

She glanced away and watched a pair of middle-aged women stroll by arm in arm, their coats open, their faces raised to the sunshine. Then a young woman, by herself, and so downcast her long neck seemed permanently twisted to the side. Poor suffering girl, Lulu thought, she's so depressed she can't lift her head.

And turning back to Tony: "How do we end up the way we do? I thought you'd become a bookseller and settle down with a bad poet."

His amusement was gratifying, but she wasn't joking.

"Most of us just go with the flow," he said. "I've been operating a long time. My contacts trust me. A lot of people depend on me."

"Going with the flow. No regrets."

"I have regrets," he said.

She looked into his face. "What's your biggest one?"

He gave her his crooked, flirtatious smile. "I wish I could make you happy."

She regarded him through the jaded light of long experience. He could have made her happy a long time ago.

"No?" he said.

"No," she said.

He patted her knee, got to his feet, looked down at her with easy affection.

"Let me guess." She stood up too. "You've got an appointment with the spoilt brat."

He pulled her into one of his hugs, engulfing her in his all-embracing warmth, and she was surprised by how comforted she felt, how sorry to see him go.

===

She began to wend her way home. Passing a row of shops, she thought to turn on her phone and a moment later it buzzed in her pocket.

"You're there," Nan said.

Lulu turned her back to the traffic. "I just ran into Tony Lloyd, believe it or not, large as life. Everything all right with you?"

"I miss you, Lu. When are you coming back?"

"Soon I think. Next week probably." The first week of May. "But tell me the truth. Am I crazy? Moving to Snow Road for good?"

"I've been thinking about that," Nan said. "Where will you put your energy? That's all I wonder about."

Lulu resumed walking, her phone to her ear.

"You don't have to know," Nan said, "you'll figure it out. And we'll welcome you with open arms." She went on, "You're coming back at a beautiful time. No bugs yet, no blackflies, but it's warming up and things are coming into bloom, the serviceberries and Canada plums."

Lulu could see the blossoms—more air than petal—hovering along roadsides and at the edge of woodlots and fields. Winter was over. Ahead of her wasn't rue Fabre, but Snow Road Station. Every step was leading her back.

Station

1

THEY WERE IN Nan's screened-in porch, safe from the ravenous blackflies and mosquitoes. Jim had come home too, taking up his summer job at the county museum in Lanark. Young man blues, Lulu thought. His laptop barely worked and his boots had holes that he couldn't find the energy to have repaired.

The three households flowed into each other, Nan's, Guy's, Bethany and Blake's. In another few weeks—when his tenants moved out—Lulu would take over Guy's bungalow. In the meantime, she stayed with Nan.

On this long warm evening in May, Blake and Bethany had come to Nan's for supper. Afterwards, Guy dropped by and found them all on the porch.

"Readers," he said fondly. "It's a distinct sound."

He went to Blake and reached out his hand, awkwardly formal, and Blake did the same. Falling back on the old male reticence, which Lulu rather admired. It was restful and it made her heart ache.

Only Bethany was without a book. "I used to be like them," she said to Guy. "I used to read two or three books a week." And why had she stopped? Because her mother told her she was too old for fantasy trash and gave her a Bible-study book to read, "And it put me right to sleep."

"That would do it," Guy said with a smile. "I've got shelves of thrillers at home. Drop by any time. I'm happy to lend."

Bethany's young face, rounded by pregnancy, was quick to light up. "I will. Thank you."

Watching her brother's gentlemanly charm and Bethany so eager to be included, Lulu thought, It takes so little. The smallest effort and barriers fall.

The evening would be memorable for her brother's openness about the past and what his confession would lead to. He said he had been thinking about their father, how mean he was to him growing up, as a young teenager accusing him of ignorance and as an older teenager just not talking to him. "I wish I could talk to him now."

"And the first thing you'd say to him?" Lulu asked.

"I'm sorry."

The look on his musing face was more philosophical than sad. "We never found a way to talk to each other. I wish I could have helped him be comfortable with who he was. Rest easy. Money doesn't matter. You've accomplished a lot."

"Fathers are complicated," Lulu said.

"So is fatherhood," Nan said, putting down her book.

And Blake looked up. "What's so complicated about it? All you have to do is be there."

Silence.

"All right," Guy said. His face opened like a door and he spread his hands wide in a simple invitation. "Here I am."

It was something Lulu would not forget, the moment when tension dissolved into a new beginning.

Later, her brother and Blake went for a walk down the lane. Blake let off steam and he listened to him, Guy would tell her afterwards. The bugs were bad, so they headed to the water and went out in his boat. Blake calmed down on the water. "We all do," Guy said, and Lulu pictured them in the middle of the lake, under the stars, talking a little but not overmuch, in the way of tough guys.

"I'm thinking of things we can do together," said Guy. "It's hard to know where to start."

"Just don't give him a chainsaw," Lulu said, and her brother laughed. "Maybe take him hunting?"

"I used to hunt," Guy said. "I can't imagine hunting anymore. I haven't got the heart to rake leaves."

And so her soft-hearted brother and his prickly son were on a new path, she told Hugh the next time she saw him. It was evening and Hugh was outside when she arrived, cleaning his trusty mountain bike. An hour later, feeling the amorous stroke of curiosity that makes you want to know every detail about the person beside you, she turned on his pillow and asked who had taught him how to ride. His father, unsurprisingly, coaching him on their street in New Orleans when he was ten years old. A boy on his dusty bike, his father trotting alongside, judging when it was safe to take his hand off the back of the seat and let his son go.

"So if you were Guy," Lulu said, "how would you get close to Blake?"

Hugh pondered. "He's going to have a child of his own pretty soon. Maybe Guy could help out. That's bound to be appreciated."

Later still, as she was leaving, she stopped in front of one of the paintings on his walls. "I love this one," she said.

"It's not mine."

It was Norma Joyce Hardy's. An unusual woman, a surprisingly good painter who had been "more than a friend."

"One of your widows," Lulu guessed, and he demurred. Not a widow. She never married. "Like you," he said.

Lulu remained in front of the painting. "I know this spot. It's the Elphin hill."

"She did a whole series." Hugh pointed to a golden disturbance at the bottom of the canvas. "Her sister died crashing into that tree."

So a peaceful painting wasn't peaceful at all. Something in the atmosphere still trembled with shock.

"I used to see a lot of her," he said. "She was spry into her eighties and always good company. We painted together. Sketching trips around here."

"You miss her."

He nodded, remembering. "She grew up in Saskatchewan during the Dirty Thirties. The sight of a flowering tree made her gasp."

Lulu gave him one of her appraising looks. "So what is it with you and older women?"

He flashed her a grin. "In the dark, what difference does it make?"

"You mean who cares about the mantelpiece when you're poking the fire?" Both of them were laughing as she turned away. "I'd hoped it made all the difference in the world," Lulu said.

A few days later, on her way back from Lanark, she made her way down the Elphin hill to the bottom of Norma Joyce Hardy's painting—the glint of crumpled fender beneath the acrylic spill of golden leaves. Coming this way she avoided her own Calvary, near the other bridge, where she had lain on her side and endured a golden shower of humiliation. Disasters keep breaking in, she thought, grabbing you with their hooks and spinning you around.

The next afternoon she forced herself to revisit the scene, pulling over, getting out of her car, staring down at the spot where she had tried to hide, like a child in full view under a table. It was barely a ditch. She raised her eyes and followed the lines of the bridge, the curving road, the distance to the old railbed. Such wild beautiful country. And she heard Nan's voice declaring, "I'm in love with this place." She was too. Even with her sordid memories, even with the sadness of seeing the village so altered from what it used to be before the highway bypassed the train station and general store, pushing their importance off to the side. But the contours were the same—no, not even the contours. All those gravel pits in the distance beyond the church. But some of its contours were the same. The quiet. The air. The remoteness. They were the same.

The name settled inside her, spreading shade and peace like a tree. Snow Road Station in the summer. You weave your life into a place and it weaves itself into you. Older women especially, she thought, older women fall in love with rivers, gardens, houses, cottages, cabins, lakes—shedding their leafy, lovely, or unlovely, earlier lives. A place that must have had bigger plans for itself in the beginning now seemed happy in its modesty—a field flower.

2

THE SULTRY JUNE days were lazier for her than for Nan, whose bookkeeping job with the county had her in Lanark even during the summer. Soon Lulu would also have to find work, but for now the rental income from her apartment kept her afloat. In the meantime, she swam morning and evening, setting off from Nan's wooden dock, heading across the small bay and back. The water would be warmer in July, cooler in August, cold again in September. She recalled a Thanksgiving years ago when she had braved the lake for all of sixty seconds, swimming with flecks of snow in the air. She wanted to be the kind of older woman who swam until ice formed on the bay. Tough and hale, like Nan.

A week later, she was putting away her clothes in the bungalow's bedroom closet when Blake walked in and interrupted her, wanting to talk. Guy's tenants had moved out earlier in the week, and she had spent the day cleaning and sorting. A late supper and now it was dusk.

Swatting away mosquitoes and a few blackflies, they took the curving path to Guy's wide dock with its openness to every passing breeze. Blake's light summer shirt glowed almost-white in the dusk and smelled of laundry soap, reminding her of the patriarch in a Mexican village, the father of forty children with innumerable women, a much-respected figure to whom all the men knelt in greeting, who had told her rather drunkenly one night how wonderful the women of Acapulco smelled: of soap rather than detergent. Palmolive, he had said to her dreamily, while in my village they all smell like Fab.

She and her nephew sat side by side on a bench on the dock as the first stars came out. She asked how Bethany was and he said fine.

"Still no contractions?"

Blake shook his head.

"No news," she said with a small smile. She waited.

"You've known Mom a long time," he said at last.

"And your father. I've known him a long time too. Forever, in fact."

"Dad—John—," he faltered. "He's the one who raised me."

"Be fair. So did your mother."

He seemed a lot younger than thirty-two, but then we're all twelve years old inside, she thought, some of the time. "You feel torn between John and Guy," she said.

"Wouldn't you?"

She batted away a mosquito. "It never bothered you that John mistreated your mother?"

He turned and looked her in the face. "I was just a kid. Sometimes he threw things, but she got angry too. I used to hide in my room."

Lulu said, "Do you know what he did to me?"

She hadn't intended to tell him, but now she told him. And despite her brief and matter-of-fact account, she felt herself shaking by the end.

"That's horrible," he muttered.

She heard Sheba barking and Guy whistling to her.

"Maybe you don't believe me," she said.

"I believe you," Blake said. "But it doesn't change how good he was to me."

"Oh, come on." She put an angry hand on his arm. "He hit your mother, he peed on me. But he was good to *you*, so it doesn't matter?"

He shook off her hand and got to his feet.

She said evenly from the bench, "You put your eggs in the wrong basket."

He said nothing in reply.

"Anyway," she went on, as much to herself as to him, "I'm glad you're giving Guy a chance. He's a fine person and so is your mother." Her eyes welled up. Dear God. Doing justice to people—it makes you cry. "It's cruel that you've never appreciated her."

"She never appreciated *me*. She never came to hear me preach. Not once."

"Did John?"

"Half a dozen times. When I lived in Philadelphia."

A boat was trolling in the distance. Lulu followed its progress and pictured a small church. Half-empty pews, dark inside, poorly lit.

"Maybe your mother did too," she said quietly. "Then slipped out before you noticed."

Blake looked down at her. "Why would she do that?"

Out of embarrassment, thought Lulu. *I thought she'd be better. An actor who would never be great.*

Blake answered his own question. "Because I disappointed her."

Lulu nodded and got to her feet. "I know I did."

It was like picking wild blackberries, she thought later of her newly belaboured state of mind. Like bare-armed combat with long brambles that rake your skin, as hard to go backwards as forwards once you've worked your way into the patch.

3

JULY ARRIVED AND a heat wave descended. Lulu sought refuge in the airiness of Nan's screened-in porch shaded by the giant maple that never got tapped in the spring. The great old trees gave no sap at all, Nan had told her, and she remembered protesting: "Say it ain't so. Even trees get too old? Even beautiful trees?" And Nan had relented, conceding that if the tree still had a lot of canopy and wasn't rotting inside, then maybe, but the best producers were eighteen to twenty inches across. Like actresses in their prime, Lulu thought. Forget the old babes. Let them retire and be their wide, comforting, uncorseted selves.

The ample porch was their summer living room, and the maple canopy an additional roof, tripling the height of the house, and sending cool breezes into every corner and ripples of light and shadow across the floors.

One afternoon Nan said, "You're seeing a lot of Blake."

"Not a lot. He drops by from time to time."

"What do you talk about?"

"Old hurts." Quoting Nan back to herself. "Old hurts and confusions."

"Whose?"

"His and mine. And yours too."

"I wish he could forgive me." Nan squeezed the fingers of one hand, then the other. "Jim does, for all my failings. Blake's never been like that. He always preferred John and made it obvious."

"Maybe you made it obvious too. Your preference. Maybe he felt judged by you."

Nan raised her face in surprise. "You think I'm judgmental?"

"You can be."

"When?"

"I guess we all are."

But Nan wanted to know. "Tell me."

Lulu hesitated, then out it came. "Your ex told me you went to a play I was in and I was so bad you didn't come backstage afterwards." She paused. "You went home and told him you thought I'd be better."

Nan's face registered the blow. The pale shock of surprise. She leaned back and expelled her breath. "I guess I did. I guess I said that."

"You told him I was an actor who would never be great."

Nan stared at the floor and shook her head. "I can't believe I said that."

Distant voices came across the water. Neighbours at the foot of the bay. They were loud and sounded happy.

At last Nan said, "I don't know what I was thinking, except there you were on stage, having a great life, and I was stuck in a crappy marriage to a crappy guy."

Lulu asked her which play it was, and Nan said, "I don't even remember. I wasn't really focused on the play, just on my old friend doing something I'd never do."

She sighed and went on, "I wanted to see you, but I didn't want to see you. I knew you'd pity me and my tiny life. So I left as soon as the play was over. I went home." After a pause, "*Hay Fever*," she said.

"'That old chestnut." She'd been Judith Bliss, the host from hell. "I hammed it up, didn't I."

Nan raised her eyes. "So now you don't trust me either."

If anything Lulu trusted her more. Nan was right. She wouldn't have had a lot of time for her conventional life. And she should have been better in the role. She had thought so at the time.

Nan said, "I've seen you be great."

Lulu looked away. "You don't have to say that."

"I mean it."

"When? And don't say *Happy Days* or I'll scream like a banshee."

"'The first time was when you played Hedda Gabler. You were magnetic. I've never forgotten."

Hedda Gabler, thought Lulu. A great role. And she had been good. Not great, but good. Because who was she trying to kid?

"I trust you," she said. "I really do. And you don't have a tiny life. You have this wonderful place. You know a million things. You have two sons."

"Neither of them happy." Nan's bleak laugh.

"They won't always be unhappy. Jim is wonderful. And Blake is coming around."

Nan removed her glasses and rubbed her eyes, and put her glasses back on. "Lu, don't let something I said when I was hurt and jealous come between us."

Lulu reached across the table and took Nan's hand in hers.

"I couldn't bear it," Nan said.

4

BETHANY GAVE BIRTH on a sweltering August 1st. She had asked Nan to be at her side in the hospital, "But don't tell my mother or she'll kill me."

Nan phoned Lulu after the birth, and later that day Lulu got in her car and drove to her brother's   "Come on, gramps," she said—and together they made the forty-minute drive to Perth, where they found the new mother in a semi-private room, propped up on pillows with the baby in her arms. Blake was perched on the windowsill. Nan was knitting in a chair.

Lulu barely noticed them, drawn irresistibly to the little creature in Bethany's arms.

"Do you want to hold her?" Bethany said.

From one set of arms to another and the newborn was nestling against Lulu's chest—the tiny red face, the eyes like slits, and the body so warm, like a wee furnace.

"Does she have a name?" Not yet, they told her.

Cradling her, Lulu listened to her peeps and murmurs, which were like music, she thought.

Guy stood at her side, a doting grandfather at first sight. "She's amazing," he said as Lulu shifted the baby into his arms. "I'm already besotted with the little squirt."

Blake left his perch on the windowsill and came over to them. He peered down at his daughter, stroked her cheek with his finger, and Guy said to him, "You've done well, you and Bethany."

Blake didn't raise his eyes, but he didn't object.

"I hope you feel as proud as I do," Guy said.

Nan had put down her knitting. "If only I'd brought my camera. You should see yourselves. You're all on cloud nine."

"Don't forget me." Bethany was reaching out to them.

Blake took the baby from Guy and settled her in the crook of Bethany's arm, and Nan suggested they leave the brand-new family for a while so they could rest and be together. Then come back tomorrow.

In the parking lot, Lulu laughed with pleasure and dashed tears from her eyes. "My God," she said, wrapping one arm around Nan and the other around Guy. "What a marvellous thing. I'm in love."

"I'm in love," she repeated to Hugh. They were on his back porch near a long-legged mix of cosmos and daisies offering up their petals to the warm evening air. "You know what they're calling her? Victoria." She raised a wry eyebrow. "I'm guessing somebody watches soap operas." Then with an air of mischief, "I think I'll call her Queenie."

It occurred to her that she had never asked Hugh if he had children of his own. She asked him now.

"None of my own," he said. "My wives already had kids when we got together." Lulu had to smile, never having asked about past wives either. "How many wives?" He held up two fingers. He wasn't in their lives anymore, he said, except for the odd visit now and again. "I'm quite happy not being the centre of anyone's life. Aren't you the same?" he said.

"You're thinking of Nan," Lulu said.

Unlike Nan, unlike Hugh, she wanted to be at the centre. Not necessarily the most important person, but important.

Holding the infant changed her body and soul. It wasn't a matter of feeling wrenched open, as she had with certain roles or lovers, but rather unfolded, without force or resistance, like a flower.

"I can't stay away," she said to Bethany. "May I hold her?"

In their only armchair she held Queenie close and listened to the little rhapsody of purrs, gurgles, bird talk. Her right hand on the back of the baby's head, her left on the whole of her tiny back, and they were like a totem pole, one figure fitting into another, but warm and alive.

Women of a certain age, she would come to think. Newborn babies and melancholy men were catnip to them.

Blake came in while she was there. "Your daughter's a little dreamboat," she said to him. "Holding her is better than a blood transfusion."

He looked openly pleased and visibly tired from taking night shifts so that Bethany could get some sleep.

Lulu observed, "Fatherhood suits you."

And Bethany, her heart in her face, said, "He loves being a father."

With her bank balance getting low, Lulu went to the liquor store in Lanark and asked for an application form. A droopy young woman with her hair at a loss sent her to the back, where Lulu spoke with another woman, older, with lofty hair coiled on top of her head and freckles covering every square inch of her busty, energetic self. A busy cynic, Lulu gathered, who complained that people with time management problems really should deal with them. "I'll be on time," Lulu promised.

That evening she played cribbage with Jim, who recalled card games with his father, with fond and luckless George who had died of cancer when Jim was fifteen. "It was a scene," he told her. "Both of us hated to lose. I remember crying with rage and beating on his chest, and all he did was laugh." They had tried Scrabble and it was worse, his father outrageous in his defence of words he made up, the two of them adamant, but George as flagrant in his sneakiness as Mr. Darling in *Peter Pan*.

Lulu said, "I'm grateful to him for one thing. You had to stop mumbling so he could hear what you were saying."

"I'd say, 'Do you hear the thrushes?' And Dad would shake his head. He couldn't hear the birds."

"Noël Coward's mother was also deaf. Did you know that? So Coward *had* to enunciate." She paused. "You'll be twenty-four soon."

"In another month."

"So far, so good," she said. But Jim went quiet. He dealt and Lulu picked up her cards and said, "A penny for your thoughts."

Jim remained intent on which cards to put into his crib. Then he admitted that he had written to Maya, his old girlfriend, a few weeks before, and when she replied he'd felt the life flow back into him. They had exchanged several messages, but this time she put a stop to it for all the old reasons: that it was too hard on him not to be loved as he wanted to be loved, and on her not to love as she wanted to love. At the end of the summer he would be back in Boston, and he didn't see how he was going to hold up, living in the same city.

Lulu remembered the small boy jamming his hands into his pockets, playing with whatever he had in there—coins, jackknife, stones, string—and talking at length about what was on his mind. She remembered thinking he might have to endure a fair bit of loneliness until he found a few quirky friends who didn't fit in either.

"Jim, I'm beating the pants off you." That drew a small smile. "Boston is big. Forget the girl." Lulu said, "Believe me. I know what I'm talking about. You'll find someone else."

"The right one? Out there just waiting for me to come along?"

"Oh, I never said the *right* one," Lulu said, and their laughter carried across the bay.

Later, he began to tell her about the history of pioneer settlers in Lanark County whose hardships appealed as much to her imagination as his. The literate Scots of Lanark, who wrote many letters, dealt with the impenetrable forest by letting in the light, which is to say, and Jim did, that in canny fashion they cut rings around tree trunks, causing the leaves to wither and fall, and the trees to die. Then at the sunny base of these tall dour cadavers, they planted potatoes and wheat.

"It's what really interests me," Jim said. "The history of places."

"Not music?" his mother asked, joining them on the porch.

"Are you disappointed?" he said.

"No, but it's a big shift. Is it what you want?" He said he thought it was. He would finish his degree in musicology, then take up graduate work in history at some point in the future. "And you won't give up the piano?" He promised that he wouldn't. Nan confessed that she loved history too, especially stories about hard times and self-sufficient people. "Do you remember asking me—you were sick and home from school—you asked me if I ever had the feeling the world was falling apart? If we should stock up on food and learn how to hunt?"

Jim's eyes lit up, amused, glad to be reminded, and his mother said, "You were always full of big unanswerable questions."

Watching their rapport, Lulu understood Blake's jealousy, and even her own. She too envied this mother and son who shared a wavelength and a love that was deep and secure.

"Does it mean you'll be closer to home?" Nan asked him. "If you're going to study local history?"

He smiled a noncommittal smile.

"I could get Hugh to look harder for a good piano," she said. "I would do that." Jim's face held back, so Nan nodded and said, "You'll do what you need to do."

5

LULU WAS ON the dock when five loons glided by without making a sound. A breeze came up. She listened to the *chuck chuck* of lapping water. Over the course of the day, the range in temperature would be like a full hand of cards. Morning breezes, midday sun, afternoon stillness, no more birdsong. Hours of buttoning and unbuttoning now that the end of summer was upon them. She wondered how many other aging, impoverished actors were scattered across the country, not necessarily wishing they had done something else with their lives, but wishing they were still wanted, still somebody.

Soon she would raise her face to more colour and bird life than she had ever imagined. Flocks of migrating warblers arrived without fanfare in early September, moving and twittering in the treetops. It astounded her how there could be nothing at all, and then something wonderful. A tiny child, with curving lips and large hands, riding on her chest. Time

spent with Queenie turned her days to gold. It wasn't that she
was meant to be a mother. She was meant, for once in her life,
to feel this tender and this untroubled about feeling so tender. It could have been a puppy, she thought, a puppy named
Queenie, but it was this morsel of human life who would call
her Lulu one day.

How alert she was. How fast her fingernails grew. How
little she slept. Her big eyes fastened on every moving thing:
shadows across the floor, ripples on the water, leaves in
the wind. In the sugar bush Lulu reached for a near branch
and pulled it low for Queenie to touch the leaves. Around
them the maples—spaced out for easier tapping and collecting—received sunlight on all sides, and the sun drew out
their yellows and oranges and reds, just as the sun's warmth
stirred the sap in the spring. The leaves changed hourly now,
like Queenie.

One morning, when Lulu and Nan were looking after her
for a few hours, Queenie gave them twenty minutes of smiles
verging on giggles. And Nan said, "She knows how to make
us love her."

This was the September when the financial meltdown cap-
sized the world. Investment banks collapsed, markets went
into free fall. Too many John Sharpes were running the
world, thought Lulu. Too many gullible schmoes had fallen
for their pitches—taking second mortgages, betting on the
housing bubble lasting forever, convincing themselves the
stock market couldn't go down the tubes. Suckers. John
Sharpe had been the dress rehearsal and now they were getting the floor show.

By this time Jim had returned to Boston to finish up his thesis on the jazz bands that toured New England dance halls in the 1920s and '30s. Ducky had moved to Montreal and theatre school with Lulu's parting words in her ear: "My darling, remember: you're the one who's going places."

And Lulu was still seeing Hugh Shapiro. They were lovers the way some people are Sunday painters: not full-time, not exclusively, but companionably and gratefully.

Jim's birthday happened the very day Lehman Brothers in New York went bankrupt. After work, Nan and Lulu phoned him from Nan's kitchen to wish him happy birthday, and when it was Lulu's turn she took pleasure in saying that his old girlfriend had been as out to lunch as Lehman's. (As indeed she herself had been wrong all those years ago when they sat in Guy's pasture and she misread his palm. It made her wonder what other corrections were bearing down.)

"So what's it like up there?" Jim said with a lift in his voice. "What's happening out the window?"

"Do you miss it, Jim?"

"I really do."

"It's beautiful," she told him, and she described the moon hanging low in the sky and the sky tinged with lavender. She told him about pulling over after dark to the flower stand at the corner of Ragged Chutes Road and slipping a ten-dollar bill into the money jar, then selecting from the pails of flowers the ten best gladiola blooms, guessing at their colours in the moonlight. Now they formed a giant bouquet on the kitchen table of yellow, purple, shocking-pink.

She told him about one of the widows who was a regular at the liquor store and had confessed that from having nobody to speak to in the morning her voice had become scratchy and thin. So she had taken to singing hymns beside her shelf of orchids, which hadn't flowered in years. And they bloomed! There were other customers she was fond of: Bill, the old regular who always replied, "Atta girl," when she greeted him; Ernest, the stooped gent from Blake's wedding with the filthy comb and magnificent head of hair, who came in every other week for his bottle of Cherry Heering liqueur. Underage lads, of course, hoping to pull the wool over her eyes.

She wanted Jim to know that Hugh had been showing her photographs of Snow Road Station as it was fifty and seventy-five years ago. "When it was wide open," Jim marvelled, taking the words right out of her mouth.

"Barely a tree," she agreed. "I guess they cut them down for firewood."

"And to pasture their cows." Jim said, "How's Queenie?"

"She's in my lap, sucking one of my fingers. Not just sucking, she's exploring with her tongue. She's got a queue of babysitters, you know. I have to elbow my way to the front."

The day before, with Queenie riding on her chest, she had been gathering a bouquet of asters and goldenrod when the long arm of an air current socked her in the nose with perfume—the air in September being sweet and pungent by turns. Butterflies rested on the road, flying up when they walked by, opening their coloured robes, their kimonos, showing everything. All around them the world was drenched with light and drunk with colour: ankle-high yellow leafiness (wild sarsaparilla, Guy had told her), knee-high bracken the colour of cinnamon, waist-high asters purple and mauve, head-high beech saplings a golden-bronze, and overhead the grand maples turning red and gold. Full sun and twenty-three degrees.

"Is it dangerous to be so happy?" she wanted to know, and Jim's gentle scoffing came down the line. But Lulu was serious. "I've never been happier," she said.

No internal clock was telling her how long it had been since her agent called, or how long since any of her begging or sarcastic emails had been answered. Here, time was the days and hours of Queenie's life. It was the length of a sunrise. A voluminous sunrise that very morning—she had opened her eyes to its glory and moved fast, heading down to the water in unlaced shoes and jacket, catching the full blast of reddish-orange and rosy-pink. Later, looking up at restless birds in the treetops, she wondered what that blue tarp was doing there, strung between the trees, and realized it was the sky, the blue sky, protecting them from rain.

6

SHE WAS HAVING early morning coffee with her brother and they were talking about the economy falling apart. Guy said, "But I've never believed in progress."

"I do. Look at us. We used to hate each other."

"You always loved me."

It was true.

He said, "We always loved each other."

That was true too. "When we weren't hating each other," she said.

His face turned pensive as he circled his mug with his hands.

"What is it?" she said. "What's wrong?"

Julie had filed for divorce. She wanted half his assets, even half his pension from all his years with the Ministry of Natural Resources. The legal papers had come to him a few days ago. He would have to sell a big chunk of waterfront to come up with the money.

It was *The Cherry Orchard* all over again. Her brother would have to break the property into cottage-lots in order to save a portion for his family.

Lulu pushed aside her mug. "Why don't you sell to me?"

He raised an eyebrow. "You've got deep pockets I don't know about?"

"I'll put my place in Montreal on the market."

His face turned grave and he studied her.

"Or," she said, "you could marry a rich widow."

"No more marriages for me," Guy said.

Now Lulu understood more than ever why so many grey-haired cashiers worked for next to nothing. They had to. She was one of them. She wasn't Madame Ranevskaya, incapable of lifting a finger to protect what she cherished from the developer's axe. She was an aging ex-actor who would save the family home.

"I'm serious," she said.

Guy looked at her, unconvinced. "Aren't you going back to Montreal at some point? Aren't you still an actor?"

"I'm happy here."

He rubbed his temples with flattened fingers, then rubbed his eyes. "What are you going to live on?"

"What I get at the liquor store. I don't need much. You're not charging me rent, after all."

"I wouldn't."

"I'll sell it this fall."

"In the middle of this meltdown? Think about it," Guy said.

Montreal real estate was its own world, she told him. Besides, the scary housing upheaval was in the States, not in Canada.

Guy looked dubious, so she took a deeper plunge. "Maybe you don't like having me around?"

"I do," he replied without hesitation. "I do want you around." He continued to frown, thinking it through. "Are you saying we divide the property?"

"We can be co-owners. But I don't really care who owns it, so long as I can stay."

"Then co-owners it is. But think about it for a while." He added, "You'll be closing the door on Montreal, you'll be stuck here in Snow Road. Is that really what you want?"

"It seems to be," Lulu said.

That night the rowdiness of the moon interrupted her wakeful thoughts (a rising moon thrusting itself through an opening in the trees and bathing her bedroom in near-daylight) and so did the commotion of late-night arrivals, young people one bay over, who played bongo drums and never went to bed.

At dawn the trees were full of birds again, moving, alighting, rustling, passing through. Mushrooms populated the path down to the water, dark-butterscotch and lacquered. That morning she swam with the fallen leaves floating on the bay. It was cold, but not achingly cold. The quiet startled her. Made her feel she should breathe it in and hold it inside herself, and not forget.

Walking back up the path, she paused to watch bouncing-babies of golden light do somersaults in the topmost leaves. Joyous bursts of colour and movement. The bungalow sat in

a field of vertical yellow, leafiness laddering up to the sky—
airy and floating and so delicate it looked almost Japanese.
The leaves really did fall one by one. Each leaf had its own
descent.

In the evening she went down to the water and gasped
at the impossible far shore—the lime-green of the grass at
the water's edge, the god-like blending of colours in the trees
above. Light seemed to be coming from deep within the leaves,
as if the colours were being cooked in hazy fats, the haziness
made not of air, but of leaves melting into the air. Up on the
hilltop the heroes of crimson and orange were baring their
chests, stabbing themselves in the heart, tossing fistfuls of
coins in the air. Such bravura performances. Such scene steal-
ers. Such hams.

All you have to do, she thought, is put yourself in the way
of beauty, put yourself into the incredible swing of it. And
her mind moved through the whole dance from sap to bud to
shade to these days of glory—these extravagant last acts—
before the trees lost everything to the wind and the rain, and
oncoming winter. Then for months on end they would go
naked, crayoned by snow. And then begin again.

She had plans for Julie's garden, neglected in the past year.
She would plant currant bushes and a plum tree. A cutting
garden. Cowslips. Anemones. Yes, there was such a thing as
progress—that this place, once the very hub of family tension, should have become so light-and-love saturated, and
that she, at her advanced age, should have learned how to
treasure it.

Guy joined her on the dock for the sunset. It came in on crashing waves of red so stupendous that he grinned and said, "*This* sailor's delighted."

Lulu wrapped an arm around her brother and they stood side by side, taking the red-sky-at-night directly on the chin.

7

THAT SATURDAY HUGH Shapiro dropped by to tell Nan about a good piano for sale at a good price. He found them all gathered in the kitchen: Queenie sleeping against Lulu's chest, Sheba similarly conked out at Guy's feet, Bethany making another pot of coffee, Nan falling asleep over a book, Blake reading the *Lanark News*. Hugh greeted everyone and bent down to kiss Lulu as if they were a couple. And in their own loose-leafed, unbound way they were.

The piano belonged to a widow, naturally. She no longer had space for it since she was moving into a condo in Perth. Her husband had been a singer, Hugh said, and the piano was a nice little Japanese upright, only twenty years old. If Nan looked after it, and the piano gods stayed favourable, it might live to be a hundred.

"I keep thinking," Nan said, but she didn't go on until prompted by Hugh. "The world is such a mess," she said, "but my own life has never been better. It makes me feel unhinged."

"That's Canada," Hugh said. "People don't believe any-thing bad is going to happen here." He went on, "Canadians are wrapped up in their personal lives. In the States they are too, but they have more traumatic lives, more to be upset about."

"I worry Obama's appeal might be wearing thin," Nan said. "Though Jim can't wait to vote for him."

Lulu looked up. "It's not wearing thin." She spoke with the confidence born of a life in theatre. "He's a great per-former. He knows how to play to huge crowds, inviting people to project their hopes and dreams and desires onto him."

He had blown poor Hillary off the stage, she thought. But you can't compete with a star by being over-rehearsed and dull.

Guy spread his hands on the table. "Our banking system is safer. More regulated. That's why we're riding things out better than in the States."

"And maybe we're not so gullible?" said Nan.

"Or maybe we're being scammed and don't even know it," Lulu said, thinking again of John Sharpe.

Hugh continued his own train of thought. "Canada used to be understated and self-deprecating, short of confidence, and that made it attractive."

"I remember," Nan said.

"Now it's taken to boasting and not caring."

"I know," Nan said sadly.

"I was talking to an old girlfriend," Hugh went on. "Her life is taking her grandkids across the country from swimming pool to shopping complex to amusement park. It drives me nuts."

"You and your girlfriends," Lulu said now. "There's no end to them."

Queenie was awake and lifting herself up in Lulu's lap. Lulu raised her to her feet and Queenie laughed her first laugh. "What day is it?" cried Lulu. "Write it down. Queenie's first laugh!"

At the end of September Lulu took several days off work and drove to Montreal to see about selling her apartment. She slept on the couch in her living room, met with realtors, took Ducky out to dinner. Once she was back in Snow Road, she filled Guy in on her trip—describing the young man who would handle the sale of her apartment, reassuring her brother that Ducky was thriving, immersed in scenes from Anne Carson's translation of *Electra* and being praised for her facility with heightened text—making it sound natural and immediate—and for being mature beyond her years.

Her brother had aged, she thought with a twinge of sorrow as she watched him nurse his glass of Scotch. He had lost weight and his something-of-a-belly was gone. No longer a youthful older man: he had become old. He should be with Nan. They should be together while they still had time.

She got to her feet and went to the window. Early October rain was coming straight down. It reminded her of something she had learned years ago that she should have known on her own. She was in the Museum of Natural History in New York, listening to a lecturer describe Native dancers in Kamchatka swaying sideways in imitation of falling snow, because, as he pointed out, snow, unlike rain, never falls straight down.

She turned and said, "Tell Nan you love her."

Guy stared at her, then shifted his eyes to the glass in his hand. Lulu couldn't tell if he was mad, or sad, or lost in thought.

She waited.

"All right," he said at last.

"All right what?"

"I'll tell her that," he said.

A few days later, on a morning when she stopped by Nan's on her way to her shift at the liquor store, she discovered Sheba stretched out on a mat on Nan's kitchen floor. Well, well, well. She knelt down and gave Sheba's ears and neck a fond and thorough workout.

Nan came down wrapped in her dressing gown and Lulu greeted her with a big grin. "Finally," she said, and Nan blushed and laughed, pushed back her loose hair, girlish, embarrassed, pleased.

Guy came down in his trousers and flannel shirt, his grey hair askew. He went to Nan at the stove and kissed her on the mouth, went to his sister and kissed the top of her head, bent down to acknowledge Sheba with pats and endearments, then ambled over to the window. "This is how to live," he said, "starting your day in beauty." He turned around and gave them a broad grin. "I feel sorry for people who don't live in nature."

"Nature? What about your sexy sister and her sexy friend?"

He chuckled. "They don't know what they're missing," he said.

Her brother was a happy man.

Later, coaxing details out of Nan, Lulu asked, "Did he ply you with Scotch?"

"He wouldn't let go of my hand," Nan said.

8

MID-OCTOBER NOW, Indian summer, and everything remaining on the lake of bays came out to meet them. A kingfisher skimming along the shore, a pair of silent loons, three otters diving down and resurfacing, then a beaver. It came within a few feet of the dock, as if delivering the mail.

That evening a few straggling mosquitoes arrived to hang off the screens.

"Whoever invented screens was a genius," Lulu said.

"Who *did* invent screens?" Nan asked.

"Mr. Screen," Guy said.

"*Mrs.* Screen," said Nan.

Her brother had met his match. Watching him and Nan tease and one-up each other, Lulu's mind went back to when they were young, the three of them. Finding each other, losing each other, finding each other again. Musical chairs, where tears were part of the game.

That night they talked about first memories and Guy pointed to Nan's woodstove in the kitchen, and said his was the sound of flames crackling in the stove and woodsmoke. Lulu said, "Samuel Beckett remembered being born. Or so he claimed later in life."

And why not? Why couldn't memories be restored to you years later, the way in old age you might recall lines from a poem learned in school, but since forgotten, or lines from a play you once knew by heart? Or an old friend's best qualities, having let yourself lapse into forgetfulness.

It would be like reaching deep into a closet, Lulu thought, and finding a coat you used to love, or a childhood toy you once treasured, and in finding them remembering them, and wondering how you ever could have forgotten.

This part of Nan's porch was an oasis within an oasis. There was a woven throw-rug under a low rough-hewn table and four comfortable wicker chairs. Nearby was the sleep-inducing sofa that Nan moved out from the living room every summer.

After the others went to bed, Lulu stayed on. She stretched out on the sofa and listened in the darkness to the barred owl on the other side of the bay, a few manic loons, some other creaturely sounds she couldn't identify.

At one in the morning she watched the lofty moon mow the lake and hills. A scythe of moonlight mowed everything flat. Nothing escapes the white reaper, she thought. And she had a sudden memory and a further thought. She remembered the August night when she had taken an inconsolable Queenie out of doors, and Queenie caught sight of the moon and her tear-stained face became rapt, her big eyes

spellbound. Then the further thought sank in that everything around her had been swung at or chopped down at one
time or another. And that living in the woods helped you
get used to things being over, because you were closer to the
living truth that soon they would be gone.

At first light it started to rain. Thunder rolled in the distance. There was the patter of drops on the roof, then more
cracks of thunder. Everyone in the big family house slept on.
Around them the trees absorbed the rain, the lake rose, the
sky emptied. The leaves became more yellow, the yellows
more orange. Always what they are—and so changed from
what they were.

—End—

Acknowledgements

Without my great editors, I would be a very dead duck. Starting with my family: My husband Mark Fried and son Ben read and improved upon multiple versions of the manuscript. My daughter Sochi read an early draft with her keen actor's eye and answered my slew of questions; all of the wonderful theatre talk we've had over the years has been grist for the mill.

The idea for the novel came from Christopher MacLehose, my British editor and publisher, who suggested that Lulu Blake as she appears in *His Whole Life* was worthy of another book; *Snow Road Station*, he thought, would make a fine title. My Canadian editor and publisher, Martha Kanya-Forstner, saw more clearly than I ever could a narrative path to the heart of the story. Melanie Little's skilful copyediting was another boon.

Sugaring folk put me in mind of "we few, we happy few, we band of brothers." Brothers and sisters, in this case, who live among the trees during the sap harvest every spring.

Carol Sissons and David Seaborn generously shared their knowledge and read sections of the manuscript, saving me from my mistakes. Warm thanks as well to Mary O'Neill, Matt Sanger, and Farley bounding through the snow. And to Robert Lee, Steve Harris, and Robert Dodge and his family.

Among theatre folk, another generous breed, I am grateful to Clare Coulter, John Cleland, Judi Pearl, Laurie Champagne, Don Hannah, and Colleen Murphy.

Frank Koller outdid himself guiding me through the world of gold smugglers and financial crooks. My thanks to him and to Vanessa Neumann, Kevin Comeau, Garry Clement, and Cal Corley.

Special thanks to Sheila McCook and Willy Blomme for rue Fabre and much else. And to Catherine O'Grady for butter cream and cake.

Although this is a work of fiction, Snow Road Station is a very real dot on the Ontario map. I thank Bev and Murray Elliott for their memories of Snow Road as it was, their deep affection for it still, and their gracious warmth. For their enticing stories about Lanark and area, I am indebted to Courtney and Gerard Garneau.

My thanks to everyone at Knopf Canada, most especially Emma Lockhart, Ashley Dunn, and designer Kelly Hill for her captivating cover (as well as artist Shannon Pawliw for permitting the use of her painting *Borderlands*).

Finally, deep thanks to my agent Jackie Kaiser, a beautiful island of sanity in these troubled times.

© Mark Fried

ELIZABETH HAY is the Giller Prize–winning author of six novels, including *Late Nights on Air*, *His Whole Life*, and *A Student of Weather*. Her memoir *All Things Consoled* won the Hilary Weston Writers' Trust Prize for Nonfiction; her story collection *Small Change* was shortlisted for the Governor General's Literary Award for Fiction. A former radio broadcaster, she spent a number of years in Mexico and New York City, and makes her home in Ottawa.